The Earl on the Train

A Potions and Passions Novella

CATHERINE STEIN

ISBN: 978-1-949862-03-4

Book cover and interior design by E. McAuley:
www.impluviumstudios.com

To Morgan, Keira, and Anya.
The journey of life is never dull with you three.
May your own travels be filled with adventure and love.

I

The Problem With Potions

London
February, 1882

Nicholas Masterson, ninth Earl of Sharpe, had not had a potion in eighteen days. Eighteen days, six hours, and twenty-seven minutes, last he'd checked.

He pressed his head to the glowing wallpaper and inhaled deeply. God, that scent. That sharp, spicy tang of serum. Potent. Alive. Magical. He wanted to lick the wall, just for a taste.

He jerked upright, biting back a curse. He was losing his mind. He ought never to have come to this party. He looked around for somewhere to go, but the whole room was papered with the awful print, phosphorescent foliage standing out in glaring contrast to the stark, black background.

All around him men and women walked about with drinks in their hands, laughing and talking, ready to dance, play cards, or otherwise indulge at the expense of their wealthy host. Money would be wasted tonight. Young Lords and Ladies would get up to a moderate amount of mischief—enough to be scandalous while avoiding ruin. Or so they hoped.

Nick glanced in the direction of the door. He could still leave. Request to meet at another time and place.

"Sharpe! Something wrong, old man? You're looking pale."

Nick frowned at the man who had spoken. The son of a peer. Younger son, not the heir. Spendthrift. They'd met a dozen times or more. The last time had been over a card game, nineteen days ago. The night Nick had witnessed a potion-addled young man relieve himself into the punch bowl in front of one hundred guests, earning a cruel nickname that would forever haunt him. The night Nick had decided to quit potions for good.

"Brief dizzy spell. Guess the welcome potion didn't agree with me," he lied.

The man nodded. Christ, what was his name? Why couldn't names ever stick in his brain the way faces and places did? Maybe it was all those damned potions he'd drunk, clouding up his mind.

"Happens," the man said, shrugging his shoulders in the indifferent manner common to so many of his social circle. "I liked it, myself. Feels a little bubbly inside, and looks to be making people chipper. That wallpaper is really something, isn't it? Lights up the whole room. What do you think they did? Mixed a potion into the ink?"

"The glowing ink is a potion itself, mixed up in much the same way an ordinary pigment would be, but incorporating aspects of a self-lighting potion, such as you might use in a garden lamp. I expect that the serum was thinned out by mixing it with warm water before it was added. This allows for a smooth mixture that could be easily spread across the surface of the paper."

Younger Son blinked several times, his mouth slightly agape. "Er… right. Excuse me." He scampered away. Didn't people know by now that you never asked Lord Sharpe a question about potions?

Nick squeezed his eyes briefly closed, fighting off the

headache. He should have stayed home working on his redecorating project, just as he'd been doing for the past eighteen days. That damned drawing room was giving him fits. Too feminine.

And, naturally, his sister had to hie off to Scotland right when he needed her. Traveling on business with her husband? What was the world coming to? That's what he got for letting her marry for love.

The corner of Nick's mouth ticked upwards. Even as miserable as he was, he couldn't help but smile thinking of Anna and her pure happiness.

He glanced around the room, searching for familiar faces he might need to avoid. Most of the men he'd called friends had laughed when he had declared he was quitting potions. Only Carsley had encouraged him. Without his support, Nick might never have gone through with it. But Carsley wasn't here tonight, and Nick was all alone in the whirl of potion-drunk guests and the unearthly glow of the luminescent wall. He sagged against it, his nostrils flaring again at the scent of the magic-enhanced paper.

"Come away from the wall, my boy."

Nick straightened up. Here was the man he'd come here to see. Thank God. A quick conversation and he could get the hell out.

"Lord Ayleston." Nick gave a polite nod to the older gentleman. At least there was one person here tonight whose name he could recall. "It's good to see you."

"And you. Would you care for a drink?"

Nick accepted the glass and took a long sniff. Brandy. With not a hint of potion. He took a long swallow. "Thank you."

"Walk with me. I hear Sir Mortimer has a beautiful library and I'd like to see it."

What Sir Mortimer really had was stupid amounts of money, earned from building a fleet of ships for the Imperial

Potions Company. His books were probably all gilded, and Nick doubted they had ever been opened.

He took another gulp of the brandy and followed Ayleston in silence.

"I imagine you're wondering why I asked you here," Ayleston said.

"Not especially."

Ayleston paused, regarding Nick with raised eyebrows. "No?"

"Well, *here* is a bit of a puzzle." Nick waved a hand at the guests mingling about them. "I wouldn't have thought this to be your sort of gathering."

"No, but it is your sort."

"Was."

"Mmm." Ayleston ushered him out the door. "I believe the library is this direction."

Nick didn't much care. They could go anywhere as long as he was away from the phosphorescent wallpaper and the potion-toting servants. He'd hold this conversation in a linen closet, if need be.

"So." Ayleston let several silent beats pass before continuing. "Why do you believe I wished to see you?"

Nick glanced over his shoulder, but the hall was empty, even of servants. "Potions are failing."

They slipped into the library, closing the door behind them. A single wall sconce burned low, casting dim shadows across the rows of pristine books.

"What makes you think that?"

Nick sank into a chair and polished off the glass of brandy. "Potions have been weaker of late. Weakening steadily, in fact. The last few months I found I was drinking more and more to achieve the same effects. I had thought my tolerance had simply gone up, but recently..." *Since I stopped drinking them...* "I've noticed other signs of weakness. Lights are dimmer. Steam cars don't go as far or as fast."

Ayleston stroked his beard. "We don't believe potions are failing."

"Oh? What then?"

"Serum is becoming scarce. Instead of raising prices, the potion makers have used less serum. Diluted their products."

"Are our sources drying up?"

"The IPC says no. In fact, they deny the existence of any problems whatsoever."

Nick tilted his glass back and forth, watching the amber droplets run along the bottom. "I can't say that surprises me. They have investors to please."

"Regardless of what they say, astute potion connoisseurs such as yourself have begun to notice this troublesome trend."

Connoisseur. Fancy French word for addict. Nick's skin crawled. He wanted to get home before he lost his nerve and sampled the refreshments here tonight.

"And?"

"Gladstone is concerned. A severe shortage puts the economy in jeopardy. We don't believe that it is yet necessary to bring this matter to the attention of all of Parliament, but…"

"But you want me to investigate."

"If you would. Your mother believes you are once again in need of an occupation."

"I have an occupation."

"She thinks you are bored."

"I'm redecorating my house."

"Personally."

"Yes."

"You are an earl."

"I am aware of that fact."

"Sharpe, peers of the realm don't move furniture and paint the walls."

Nick shoved himself up and out of the chair. "I didn't paint the walls. I stripped them. The color in the dining room was too bright and not at all conducive to good digestion. We can eat in the breakfast room until it's redone." He turned toward the door. He was going home. Ayleston's project and his mother's meddling could be left until morning.

"Nicholas," Ayleston sighed.

He glanced back. "Yes, Uncle?"

"Your country needs you. And I think you could use the distraction."

Nick took a deep breath. Perhaps his country did need him, but his higher duty was to family. And maybe getting out of town would do him good. Lord knew he needed all the help he could get. "Very well. Send me the details. I will be ready by noon tomorrow."

He strode from the room without another word, walking directly out of the house to his waiting carriage. Inside the vehicle, he sank back against the cushions and withdrew his pocket watch. The hands and numbers glowed, illuminated by the same magic pigment that lit Sir Mortimer's wall.

Eighteen days, seven hours, thirteen minutes.

II

The 7:25 to Dover

"W_{AIT!}"

Miss Ida Quimby flew down the platform, her monstrous carpetbag clutched in both arms, heedless of the chaos left in her wake.

She couldn't miss this train. How had this happened? She had left so much extra time. But then the traffic… Why had there been so much early morning traffic? Was the world conspiring against her?

The porter pulled the step stool away from the train and climbed aboard.

"Wait! Please!"

This wasn't happening. She needed this. Her livelihood depended upon it. Missing this train meant missing the packet ship, and she couldn't afford to pay for two new tickets. She had budgeted this trip down to the penny.

The porter reached to place a chain across the steps. The train whistle shrieked notice of departure.

"Stop!"

The porter froze. He had heard her.

"I'm here! I'm coming!"

Ida's legs burned. The train lurched. Almost there. Only a few steps. Her heart pounded in her chest, blood roaring in her ears. With her last ounce of strength, she heaved the carpet bag up onto the train and leapt after it.

The porter gave a squawk of alarm. "Good heavens, miss, are you quite all right?"

Ida lay on her belly, chest heaving, the cold metal of the floor pressed against her cheek. Her feet dangled out over the steps, and the entire station could probably see her petticoat and stockings. But she was on the train.

"Yes." She took a deep, steadying breath. "Yes, I am quite well, thank you. If I might just have a moment?"

"Er… y-yes. Of course, miss."

I'm here. I made it.

Ida took a few seconds to catch her breath and let the panic subside before sitting up and taking stock of herself. Her hair was a disaster and she had lost her bonnet, but all else seemed to be in order. Her parasol still jutted from the carpetbag, unharmed, and there were no tears in her dress or her stockings. The pale pink fabric of her skirt appeared miraculously unstained. She rose, dusted herself off, and picked up her belongings.

"Would you like me to take your bag for you, miss?"

"No, thank you. I prefer to keep my things with me."

Holding the unwieldy bag in front of her, she stepped into the train car and set out to find a seat. Her arms ached. The bag wasn't meant to be carried about by a smallish woman, especially stuffed full as it was, but Ida didn't dare relinquish it. Too much had already gone wrong today. She wouldn't risk lost luggage.

The other passengers stared and frowned as she walked by. Once she found a seat, she would have to make some attempt to repair her coiffure. There was no sense spending the next three hours looking like a wild hellion who had leapt, screaming, onto the train. Even if she was one.

Ida moved on to the next car, lurching a little under the weight of her luggage. This one appeared as crowded as the last, but surely she would find a seat soon. It was only natural for the cars nearer the front to fill up first. She continued on.

And on.

Was half the city going to Dover? There were at least a dozen stops along the way. Where on earth would they put all the other passengers?

She pushed through yet another doorway and sighed in relief. There, perhaps a third of the way down, was an empty seat. She rushed ahead, eager to rest her tired legs.

"Is this seat..."

She froze, her words hanging unfinished in the air. The other occupant of the seat was a man. And not just any man. A very large man, tall and strapping, with a hard jaw shadowed by stubble. His dark hair had a slight wave to it that he hadn't bothered to tame with oil. He glared down at his pocket watch with a scowl so intense that Ida feared he might crush it in his fist. Or throw it at someone.

"Comfortable? No."

Ida jerked, her body awakening from its stupor. Was that a joke? His voice was so low and gruff that she couldn't tell.

"But it is unoccupied," he added.

She breathed a sigh of relief. "Oh, good."

She dropped the carpetbag onto the ground and pushed it in front of the seat, then sat as best she could. The bag took up most of her legroom, so she perched on the edge of the seat, ankles crossed, her feet sticking out slightly into the aisle. Her overcoat she placed atop the bag, folded as best she could manage. The train was too warm to wear it, or perhaps she had yet to cool down from her unplanned exertions.

The big, handsome man spared her a glance. Eyes the color of amber looked her up and down, then turned to the window.

He snapped his watch shut with less violence than she would have expected, given the look of utter hatred he had given it moments before.

She studied him for a moment. He wasn't taking more than his fair share of the seat, yet she had a strange sense that he was somehow invading her personal space. Was it the way he held himself so stiffly? Or his unusually broad shoulders? Perhaps it was his aristocratic profile. He looked like a man of importance. Which was ridiculous, considering that these were second class accommodations. He could hardly be more important than she was. A man of business, most likely. His charcoal frock coat looked to be well-used, though clearly of high quality. Ida approved of that particular philosophy. Save your pennies and buy the best and it would serve you well for a long time.

Ida began pulling pins from her hair in preparation for redoing it. Without a mirror, she would need to keep it simple.

"Good morning," she said to her seatmate. "I'm Ida Quimby, and it's a pleasure to make your acquaintance. I hope you had a better start to your day than I did."

His head turned slowly, and he stared at her for a long, silent moment. "I wasn't so late to the train that I needed to do my hair in public, so there is that."

"Ah, but you didn't shave. And I'm not certain you did anything to your hair at all. It almost looks as if you simply rolled out of bed and smoothed it down with your fingers."

"Imagine that."

Ida thought she caught the merest hint of a smile tugging at the corner of his mouth, but he looked away again before she could be certain.

"Might I at least have the pleasure of your name?" she asked. "We are to be together for the next three hours, and it would be more agreeable if I knew with whom I was conversing."

"Nick Masterson. Though I have no interest in conversation, so little good it will do you."

"It's a pleasure to meet you, Mr. Masterson. I'm certain you will wish to converse later on, even if you don't now. What else is there to do on our journey? Or have you brought a book?" She glanced around but didn't see one. "Do you have a favorite author? I'm quite partial to Mrs. Gaskell, though she is not so popular now as in my mother's day. I'm afraid I fancy John Thornton rather terribly, and it is entirely possible that he has ruined me for any real man."

Mr. Masterson shifted in his seat, turning almost sideways to look at her. "Pity."

Ida stabbed the last of her pins into her hair. "There's no need to be so sarcastic, sir. Is it the early morning start? I know some people have difficulty rising with the sun."

"The sun that is only just now rising?"

"Quite. I suppose we all had to rise before it, didn't we?"

"Indeed. And seeing as I won't consider it morning until about the time we arrive in Dover, I must beg you to leave me in peace."

"Yes, of course."

Ida folded her hands in her lap and pinched her lips closed. In the silence, the clacking of the train wheels became a roar in her ears. All her travel guides were at the bottom of her bag, inaccessible. She ought to have placed them on top for easy access, but she had expected the thrill of travel to be enough to keep her occupied. Her fingers twitched, and she shifted in her seat. Only three hours to Dover. How bad could it be?

Each little sound in the compartment pricked at her ears. A yawn. A cough. The rustle of a newspaper. She held out as long as she could.

"Well, it looks as though the weather will be pleasant today."

If she couldn't talk to him, she would talk to herself.

"I'm glad for it," she went on, "because it should make for an easy voyage across the Channel. I would hate for my first visit to France to begin with a bout of *mal de mer*. Are you continuing on to France, Mr. Masterson?"

Oops.

He glared at her. His poor pocket watch. Surely it had cracked under that same rock-hard gaze. Ida smiled back at him. She wouldn't crack. She had four older brothers.

"Miss… Whatever-Your-Name-Is… I have a fearsome headache and was awakened at an ungodly hour. If this continues, I don't think I will be able to endure your presence, even if you do smell like strawberries."

"Oh! You noticed! Do you like it? It's my newest scent. I used both strawberry and strawberry blossom, and I believe I have at last gotten the proportions right. The floral and the fruit together are a rather delicate balance, you see, and…"

He slumped against the wall and closed his eyes. "Have at it, Miss Strawberries. I surrender."

III

Mal de Mer

Nɪᴄᴋ ᴄʟᴜᴛᴄʜᴇᴅ ᴛʜᴇ ʀᴀɪʟ, willing the steamer to go faster. Or to turn around and go home. Anything to end the agony.

You can end this.

The thought sparked an acute awareness of the many vials tucked into the pockets of his coat. One swallow and he could settle his heaving stomach.

No.

He wouldn't ruin this. He wouldn't throw away almost twenty days of self-restraint on a mere bout of seasickness. Even if it might actually be killing him.

Had it been this bad when he was a child? He remembered a lot of vomiting, but not how it had felt. If he had, he might have told Ayleston to go jump in the Thames.

"Oh, Mr. Masterson! You are traveling to France, after all!"

The cheerful voice stabbed into his brain.

"Oh, bloody hell."

This mission couldn't possibly have begun more poorly. He had anticipated the early morning and the cramped accommodations, and even the sleepless night that often preceded this sort of venture. What he hadn't anticipated was that the most beautiful woman he'd ever seen would plop down into the seat beside him—along with a carpetbag the size of a small elephant—and talk at him for three hours straight.

He didn't want to like her. He didn't want to like anything at all just now, when he was exhausted and ill and anxious about carrying potions on his person. He wanted to be surly and angry at the world. But she had barged into his misery with her perfect smile and her bubbly personality, and, God help him, he liked it. Almost enough to improve his mood.

Almost.

He should have stayed home and worked on the drawing room.

"Is the view nice from here?"

She came up to stand beside him, and he risked glancing away from the horizon. Who was this woman? She was dressed like a debutante, all pink and ruffled. Even her wool overcoat was pink, with white fur at the neck and wrists. Pink lace gloves covered elegant hands, and a matching parasol rested on her shoulder. She was young, at most the same twenty-three years as his sister. Yet she had no maid, no chaperone. No mother or sister. Not even a scowling older brother or a daft uncle.

"You look a bit pale," she said, her delicate, blond brows crinkling together in a frown. "Are you unwell? Could I fetch you something?"

"No. Thank you."

Nick fixed his gaze back on the horizon. Damn, but he felt like hell. Nausea rolled over him in unrelenting waves, turning his stomach in knots. The constant rocking of the boat made him lightheaded and unsteady on his feet.

"Have you tried ginger root? It comes highly recommended. Or perhaps you would feel better sitting down? I would be happy to help you find a seat."

"No." He'd come up here for the fresh air. The enclosed passenger compartment only made it worse.

"Well, I feel terrible not being able to help. Er… not so terrible as you feel, no doubt, but…"

"I'm fine." Why did she have to be so damn nice? How could she tell that he wasn't always a miserable, scowling curmudgeon?

"Of course." He could hear the disbelief in her words. "Perhaps I will simply distract you from the tedium of the journey, then. You are the only person I know aboard this ship, after all. What shall we talk about? France? Have you been before? Is it your final destination? I have never been out of England, myself, and I'm greatly looking forward to it, though I'm just passing through."

Nick shut his eyes and concentrated on her voice. To his continued annoyance, it had a pleasant lilt that he found soothing, even if her words did tumble out at an alarmingly rapid pace. Her accent suggested that she was a woman of education and wealth, which again made him wonder what she was doing traveling second class alone.

The fruity scent of her perfume infiltrated his nostrils. The fragrance was neither cloying nor acrid, and she had applied just the right amount. She was some sort of perfume expert, based on her hour-long talk on tinctures and essences on the train. He'd missed most of it, trying to focus on the task his uncle had assigned him and the questions he needed to ask along his journey.

The men in Dover had been singularly unhelpful. None of the dock workers he'd spoken to could even identify a potions shipment, and the customs officials had glared at him as if he'd been a smuggler. Even throwing around his title had gotten him nowhere. Unshaven and dressed in his less-than-pristine coat, they probably hadn't believed him.

No matter. He hadn't expected to learn anything of

importance in Dover anyway. What mattered were his findings on the continent and, ultimately, in India.

"...Have such an opportunity, so I decided to allow myself two days of perusing the perfumeries and seeing the sights."

Nick opened his eyes, trying to process her words. "I'm sorry, two days in Paris?"

"Yes, that's correct. I'm taking the three p.m. train from Calais today. It won't arrive until after eleven, I'm afraid."

He grimaced, and not from his illness. "Yes, I know."

"Oh! Are you taking the same train?"

"I am."

"Wonderful! It's so nice to travel with someone I know. I wasn't at all certain how it would be, traveling. I imagine it's not the easiest thing, to make friends on a train, but it seems to have worked out rather well, don't you think?"

"Miss..."

Damn. What was her name? She had only said it the once that he could recall, and of course it had washed right over him like these hellish waves that lapped at the side of the ship.

He forged ahead regardless. "Putting aside the fact that a few hours' journey together on public transport hardly constitutes a friendship, am I correct in my belief that I am the closest you have to a companion during your travels?"

"Well, yes. So far."

"And you are not meeting any friend or relative upon your arrival in Paris?"

"No. I'm staying at a hotel. The arrangements have already been made. I have my copy of *Bradshaw's Guide*. Have you used it? It has travel tips, train schedules and pricing, hotels, ads for useful products and services..."

"I've seen it, yes. But to be clear, you intend to wander the city *alone* for two days?"

"That had been my plan, yes."

"Bloody hell."

Her cheeks turned the color of her dress. "Mr. Masterson, really!"

"I beg your pardon. I'm feeling rather unwell just now, and my mind is not where it should be."

"Oh! Yes, of course. I'm so sorry. Is there anything I might do for you?"

Nick leaned on the rail, the churning in his belly a fraction less than it had been before the distraction of Miss Strawberries. She'd been right about that, irritatingly enough.

"Simply keep talking about... something." He waved a hand. "The sights you wish to see in Paris, perhaps."

"Oh, well, I do wish to go to the Louvre, though I have time to see only a fraction of its collection, and..."

Nick made a mental list of places as she rattled them off. It would be damned awkward, escorting her around while trying to see to his own business, but there was nothing to be done about it. No way in hell was he letting an innocent young woman with no traveling experience dash about the continent all on her own. Unscrupulous louts would take one look at those spun-gold tresses and sky-blue eyes and leap to ply her with every seductive trick in their arsenals.

Or was that what she hoped for? She seemed a forthright and self-possessed woman. Perhaps she was rebelling against an overprotective family, or fleeing the promise of a passionless marriage. This was her escape. Her chance to live only for herself. It would explain the disparity between her upper class clothing and her second class fares.

If that were the case, Nick would be best served to keep his distance. Some family member would be hot on her trail. Being caught alone with her would lead to accusations of all manner of licentious behavior.

And if he was going to be accused of doing indecent things to those plump, pouty lips and that delectable body it had damn well better be because he was guilty of every single charge laid at his door.

He had poor choices, all around. Risk an angry relative? Leave her to possible danger and ruin? To the pleasures of some other man?

Nick spoke, sealing his fate. "I will be in Paris a few days on business. Perhaps we might go about together."

"Oh! That would be…" The strawberry blush returned to her cheeks. "Terribly improper. But very pleasant, I think. Thank you."

"You're welcome." He half choked on the words, as an especially large wave rocked the ship. His insides lurched. "Oh, God."

"Let me get you something. A damp handkerchief, at least, to cool your brow. You look to be… perspiring."

Nick leaned over the rail in case his breakfast made a sudden reappearance.

"I may be dead before you return."

Lace-covered fingers trailed down his arm. "Never fear! It's only another hour or so before we make landfall."

Nick choked back a mouthful of bile. "Marvelous."

IV

Carpe Diem

Iᴅᴀ ᴄʀᴜᴍᴘʟᴇᴅ ᴛʜᴇ ᴛᴇʟᴇɢʀᴀᴍ in her fist. How dare he? How dare he rebuke her as if she were a little child? After all the money she had spent to send a lengthy and informative telegram, *this* was his response? Demanding. Demeaning. Obnoxious.

She uncurled her fingers and smoothed out the paper, looking over the note a second time.

Do. Not. Come. Here. -A

As if she were in the wrong. As if it hadn't been *his* broken promise that had forced her to this.

Ida could feel the indignant heat in her cheeks. She turned red at the slightest provocation.

She took a calming breath and poured another cup of tea. Folding the telegram carefully, she tucked it into the small purse tied at her hip. She wouldn't let him get the better of her. She would press on. Her future depended on it.

Tomorrow she would send another message. A shorter one. Just long enough to convey her resolve. Today, though, was for her pleasure and she wouldn't let him ruin it with his high-handed response. Today, she would soak up the sights and sounds and smells of Paris, fill her soul with them, and create memories to treasure for a lifetime.

Or, she would if Mr. Masterson ever decided to show up. He had promised to breakfast with her, but she had already eaten and finished most of her pot of tea, and he hadn't even so much as sent a note. His hotel—several steps up from her own modest lodgings—wasn't especially far away. A few minutes by foot, at most. Perhaps he had changed his mind and deserted her. All morning she'd been sitting in the dining room, watching the other guests come and go. Was she a fool to wait?

She sipped her tea and flipped through her *Baedeker's Guide*, reviewing her marked pages. The perfumeries listed were well chosen, in her opinion. Five of them were on her agenda for today, and another three tomorrow. The weather this morning was fair, so time strolling outdoors would suit her, and hopefully the evening would afford her the opportunity to take in a show. Opera was beyond her budget, but the guide said that Paris had more than forty theaters. The true difficulty would be in choosing among so many.

"Good morning!"

Ida's head snapped up at the sound of the voice that was familiar and yet not—an odd, cheery transformation of the low growl she had come to associate with Nick Masterson.

"Er, good morning to you," she stammered.

Their eyes met and he flashed a smile at her. His amber eyes were warm today, almost liquid, with a hint of sparkle. Her tea sloshed in her suddenly unsteady hand. Goodness, was he handsome when he smiled. A small tilt of his mouth and he was five times finer than when he scowled. Which was quite something for a man who possessed the loveliest scowl she had come across in all her three-and-twenty years.

He appeared well-rested. Perhaps that was the reason for his sudden good cheer as well as his tardiness.

Masterson slid into the seat beside her—though the table was otherwise unoccupied—putting his large frame scandalously close to her. This was Paris, she reminded herself. Here, unmarried and unchaperoned men and women could dine together and whisper intimacies across the table with little fear of word reaching their respectable families back home.

Not that she intended intimacies of any sort with a stranger she'd just met. Certainly not.

Mr. Masterson flicked a wrist at the nearest waiter in what appeared to be a well-practiced gesture. The man scurried over to take his order.

"Bring me whatever the chef says is best today, a strong pot of coffee, and more tea for the lady."

"*Oui, monsieur.*"

"*Merci.*" Masterson glanced at Ida. "Do you need anything further? It appears as though you have already eaten."

"Nothing further, thank you." When the waiter dashed off to do his bidding, she added, "Of course I have already eaten. It is half past ten!"

"Yes. A civilized time to rise, if I do say so myself."

"I was up at eight."

"Were you? Dashed peculiar."

"What is peculiar, Mr. Masterson, is your keeping the hours of an idle gentleman. I thought you said you were in town on business?"

He chuckled. "My business is rather peculiar, in fact."

"Oh?" She leaned closer. "Tell me more."

He inhaled deeply, closing his eyes for a moment. "You are fruity again this morning. Blackcurrant today? With notes of citrus and something floral. Lovely."

Ida straightened before his nearness could cause her to flush again. "You have an excellent nose, Mr. Masterson."

"I'm something of a potions specialist. Not making them, mind you, but studying them. Small differences in taste and smell can signal large differences in effect, and I have trained myself to recognize such things."

"Excellent. I imagine you will enjoy our stops at perfumeries, then." She pushed her guidebook toward him. "If you would take a look at the pages I have marked and use your knowledge of the city to plan an efficient route for today's sightseeing? I would like to get through as many things as possible."

One dark eyebrow arched. "I believe I'm beginning to understand you. Just as you pack as many words as possible into every conversation, you fill your day with as many activities as you can. I imagine this is your definition of leisure."

She fought a frown, not certain if he was mocking her. "And what is *your* definition?"

"If I should ever find myself at leisure, I will let you know."

"You prefer to keep busy, then?"

"It's a necessity. I'm easily bored. Ask anyone in my family."

"I don't know your family." The scandalous reality of their friendship hit Ida so suddenly that she flinched. She knew next to nothing about this man. Only his name, his discerning nose, and his predisposition for seasickness. For all she knew, he had a wife and children back home. Or enormous gaming debts. He could even be a criminal fleeing justice.

"Nor do I know yours. Aside from your knowledge of perfumes, you have told me very little about yourself."

"True. Perhaps that is the natural way of things when two people meet on a train. Our lives intersect for a time in the course of our travels, but our pasts are behind us and our futures will diverge when our routes do. It is a fleeting relationship, but I hope a worthwhile one."

He stroked his jaw, which was clean of stubble this morning. "An interesting observation. Shall we agree, then, not to dwell on where we come from or where we are going, but simply to enjoy what time we have?"

"Yes, let's."

She extended her hand, and he clasped it to seal their agreement. The warmth of his palm started a tingle running up her arm. Their eyes locked, and the handshake lingered.

Her breath caught in her throat. He had to be a rogue with half-a-dozen mistresses. A seducer hopping across the Channel to avoid the angry fathers of his illicit paramours. A scoundrel for certain. Everyone else on the train to Dover had known to keep away from him.

Ida withdrew her hand, her skin burning where he had touched her. No pasts. No questions. Only now.

She waved a hand at her guidebook. "So, Mr. Masterson, where shall we go first?"

La Ville Lumière

*Y*OU *HAVE AN EXCELLENT NOSE, Mr. Masterson.*

A curse, perhaps, more than a blessing. Nick could identify different areas of town by scent alone. Here, the smooth glow of the potion lamps gave way to flickering gas lights, the smoky smell of their impure fuel prickling his nostrils. He took a step closer to Miss Strawberries and her exquisite perfume.

"The Folies Bergère, then?"

Nick had helped her narrow down her choice of theaters by recommending only those noted for serving potions. She had selected one and seemed determined to stick with it.

"Quite. The playbill advertised acrobatics and comedic operetta tonight, and admission is only two francs."

Her scrupulous budgeting fascinated him. She had recorded every purchase throughout the day in a little notebook, comparing each one to her list of expected expenses. Was money so tight for her? And why? Somehow he had managed to keep to their pact not to pry into her life, though these and so many other questions nagged at him.

"I must warn you that the entertainment may be bawdy at times. Salacious jokes and revealing costumes."

"Well, of course! This is Paris, after all. I expect to see the legs of can-can dancers and hear songs full of inappropriate lyrics."

Laughter bubbled up inside him. "Right. Carry on, then."

A short time later, Nick saw her settled in a seat with a reasonable view, enjoying her wide smile and excited chatter. He placed a glass of champagne in her hand and tipped his hat to her.

"Enjoy the show, Berries. I will see you at the next intermission."

"Wait, where are you going? And what did you call me?"

"I have business to attend to, I'm afraid."

"Business? Here?"

"Indeed." Her night might be nearing its end, but his was just beginning. "I will see you shortly."

"Mr. Masterson…"

"I won't desert you. I promise."

Nick strode off, hoping she wouldn't follow. To his relief, she stayed put. She'd insisted on paying her own entrance fee, and he expected she didn't want to waste her two francs.

While most of the crowd took to their seats to watch the entertainment, he wandered about, noting the frequency of potion use and surveying the bars where the drinks were mixed. He hadn't patronized this particular establishment before, but it was much like other places he had been, full of people who wished to escape reality for an evening. Potion sales were booming.

The customers, he noticed, showed a marked preference for certain barmaids over others. Unusual. Any mixer skilled enough to get and keep a job here ought to be able to handle the basic potions most patrons would request. Special requests were handled in a separate location by the more talented girls. Or so it had been the last three or four times he'd visited Paris. Ayleston may have been right to send him here. Things weren't as they should be.

Nick waited for a lull in the activity, then approached one of the most popular barmaids.

"Good evening, monsieur. Would you like a drink?"

He made a quick perusal of the woman herself. Her dress had a square, low-cut neckline, as expected for anyone in her line of work, but she neither flaunted her figure nor squirmed beneath his gaze. Her posture was confident, her brown eyes intense. A true professional.

"Yes, please. A stamina potion. Conventional, not amatory. I need to remain alert this evening."

"Until what time?"

Nick's brow furrowed. "I beg your pardon?"

"Until what time do you wish the potion to last?"

He had never heard a potion mixer ask such a question. It wasn't uncommon to differentiate between a short duration potion or an all-nighter, but requesting a particular length of time was unheard of. Did this woman really make her potions to such exacting specifications?

"Four a.m." His typical bedtime.

She looked him over, judging his size and fitness, no doubt. "And will you be engaging in any vigorous activities during this time?"

"Not likely. Walking and enjoying the entertainment." He waved a hand at the theater behind him.

The barmaid nodded and set to work. He watched her hands as she measured and mixed ingredients with the speed and precision of a true master. Hers was a rare talent. Nick could recall only twice when he had witnessed similar displays of skill.

In seconds, his potion was complete and she held it out to him, a slight smile touching her lips. This woman was justly proud of her abilities.

Nick lifted the glass to his nose and sniffed. Beyond the intoxicating scent of serum, he could sense the quality of both the ingredients and the mixing.

Perfect.

His head swam. Would it taste as good? Would it last, as she claimed, until the requested time? His nose could detect no weakness, no sign that potions here weren't as strong as ever.

"Does it meet with your approval?"

"I believe so. I've had trouble of late with potions that lacked their customary potency, but this one smells just right."

"You will never find my potions lacking."

Confident. He liked that. She had spirit, this woman, despite her miserable job. "And the potions of the other girls?"

"I can't speak for them. I do my best. I trust others to do the same."

She was undoubtedly the best here. He would have to compare her potion with potions from some of the other mixers. That would give him a better picture of the situation. He took another sniff of the potion, pulling that sharp, spicy essence deep into his lungs. How much could one tiny sip hurt? It would be useful for comparison.

The moment the liquid touched his lips, he knew he'd made a terrible mistake. The craving hit him with all the force of a thunderbolt, burning through his veins to the very marrow of his bones. He downed the entire glass, reveling in the feel of the wild, tangy magic flooding his mouth and coating his throat.

Fuck!

The potion's effect was immediate. His eyes opened wider, his back straightened. Any lingering exhaustion from a day matching the mad pace of his companion's sightseeing vanished, lost beneath the power of the drug.

"Can I get you anything else?" the barmaid asked.

Yes. More. Everything.

Nick tossed some coins on the bar and staggered backwards. "No. No, nothing."

He shoved the empty glass onto a tray of similar ones, hands shaking, mind reeling. What had he done? He pulled out his pocket watch to check the time. The potion-lit numbers mocked him.

Zero days, zero hours, zero minutes.

He stumbled through the music hall, his legs carrying him involuntarily toward another bar. He needed another potion. The sort that made him not care. The sort that made him forget that his father had died and none of Nick's so-called friends understood how much it hurt when they called him by his new title. A potion that blunted the awesome terror of responsibility thrust upon him as a lad of only nineteen, when he'd become the sole protector of his mother and baby sister.

Nick jerked to a halt a few steps short of the bar.

Pull yourself together, Masterson.

He was no longer a boy, and his sister wasn't a baby. She was married, happily, to a good man. The estate was in capable hands, his investments sound. His mother's future was secure. The only thing he'd fucked up was himself.

Nick sucked in a lungful of air and exhaled slowly. He had a task to complete here. Something to focus on. These jobs for his uncle had been his escape, once. A way to be simply Nick Masterson, and leave Lord Sharpe behind. Somewhere along the way they had lost their appeal.

He stepped up to the bar, still feeling the burn of the stamina potion in his veins. He was alert and full of energy. No sense in wasting his time brooding.

"*Bonsoir, mademoiselle.*"

The barmaid waggled her eyebrows and leaned forward to display her décolletage. "Well, hello, handsome Englishman. My name is Marie. What can I do for you?"

"A stamina potion, if you please. Conventional."

She grinned up at him as she gathered ingredients. "No plans for a night of *amour*, monsieur?"

"I'm afraid not."

"Alas. Well, if you change your mind, you know where to find me."

Marie mixed up her potion with the same speed as the expert barmaid, and handed it over to him, letting her fingers trail over his. Nick couldn't tell whether she was selling her favors, or merely a lusty woman who wanted a romp.

He sniffed at the potion, fighting the urge to drink it like he had the last one.

"Satisfactory?"

"Yes. It's quite good." Excellent, in fact. But not perfect.

"Yet you are frowning and not drinking."

"I don't want to drink it." The corner of his mouth quirked in a wry smile at the words that were both true and false. He set the potion on the bar, clenching his fists to keep from picking it up again. "I needed it for comparison."

Marie's eyes drifted across the room. "My friend Elle will win every time in such a comparison. At least among those with potions knowledge. But I can best the other girls. This potion will serve you well."

"I don't doubt it." Nick tossed a few coins on the bar and leaned against it, letting his eyes rove over Marie's pretty, petite figure. "Tell me, *ma chérie*, does everyone flock to you and your friend? You two seem popular." He glanced over his shoulder at a group of men and women hanging behind him, waiting for him to move on. "Which could be due to other factors." His gaze once again dropped to her neckline. "But I think it's your potions skills."

Her eyes narrowed. "What do you want, Englishman?"

Damn. He was a terrible flirt. Subtlety had never come naturally to him. He tried for honesty instead. "Are potions getting weaker? Are the serum supplies running low?"

"My potions are good. I cannot speak for the others.'

Almost the same reply as her friend. That told him enough. He nodded and straightened up. "Thank you. Have a pleasant night."

Nick visited two more potion mixers, requesting the same stamina potion and confirming his suspicions. The less popular barmaids served weaker potions. He needed only a single whiff to detect the lack of potency. The potions would work, but not as well and not as long. They were inferior to what he had encountered on previous visits to Paris. And not because the mixing was done poorly. These women were competent. Far better than average. Only the experts could hide the shortage. That wouldn't last if the supply dwindled further.

He took a circuitous route back to his neglected seat, steering clear of Elle the barmaid and her exceptional potions. His body still hummed with energy and itched for more. Catching the scent of one of her mixtures might send him over the edge. He sank down beside Miss Strawberries and allowed himself to check his pocket watch.

Zero days, zero hours, twenty-two minutes.

"What's wrong?" Worried blue eyes looked up at him. "Trouble with your business?"

"Of a sort. I think I will manage. A distraction would be welcome."

Distract me. Please distract me.

"Oh, well, the show is quite good. You will enjoy it."

He breathed in her fruity scent and smiled at her frilly, pink dress. She was his distraction. No singing or dancing needed. She was a feast for his senses. Her rosy cheeks and the light in her eyes provided a soothing balm for the gnawing hunger in his soul. Her musical laughter drowned out the nagging voices in his mind, and her delicious scents made him hungry for something more than oblivion. Would she taste equally divine? How could she not?

His cravings remained, and the grief, but she shone through his darkness like the moon on a cloudless night. What the hell would he do when she left Paris?

A fleeting acquaintance wasn't good enough. Where was she headed? He had to know. He had to draw this out as long as possible. Had to kiss her to discover if what he suspected was true—that the taste of her surpassed any potion known to man.

She giggled at a bawdy joke, and he edged closer, feeling her warmth, bathing in her laughter, filching all he could of her joy. He stayed by her side until well past midnight, when he at last saw her safely to her hotel before returning to his own.

Alone in his bed, he stared up at the ceiling, pondering what he had learned and what he still needed to discover. Thinking of her. Savoring and despising the power of the stamina potion still coursing through him.

At three fifty-nine a.m., Nick Masterson yawned.

One minute later, he was sound asleep.

<h1 style="text-align:center">VI</h1>

<h1 style="text-align:center">*'Til it's Over*</h1>

WHY DID THIS DAY have to end? She should have scheduled one more night in Paris. Why hadn't she scheduled one more night? She could have tweaked the budget to do that. A few cheaper meals. Forgoing the much faster first class sleeper train. If only she'd known.

But who could have guessed that it would take a trip to Paris to find the sweetest man in all of England?

Because Ida was one-hundred percent certain that's what he was. Even if he were a rake, a criminal, or—worst of all—married, Nick Masterson was sweet as her favorite blackberry trifle.

True, he had a tendency to growl, he detested mornings, and he used foul language—he had uttered several words that didn't bear repeating when she had banged on his door at eight o'clock that morning—but none of that could conceal his sugary interior.

All yesterday and all today he had catered to her every whim. He'd taken her for luncheon at a wonderful cafe she never would have found on her own, then steered her through the crowd at the Louvre to gawk at some of her favorite art. He'd even expressed interest in her perfumery. He'd never once complained about her furious pace or her constant chatter. Strangely enough, he seemed to like listening to her talk. Most people nodded politely and then did their best to escape her conversations. Or simply ignored her.

When he was neither tired nor seasick he was cheerful, witty, and kind. He smiled at children, petted dogs, and gave up their cab to an older couple when a bit of a drizzle started up. He was wonderful.

And in a mere two hours she would get on her next train and never see him again. A worthwhile relationship it had been, but all too fleeting. At least they would have one more meal together before the end.

While he took their outerwear to be checked at the coatroom, Ida stopped at the hotel desk to check for messages. Sure enough, a new telegram awaited her from Alfred. She unfolded the paper slowly, expecting another rebuke.

Don't come here. Don't write again. This is the last I will say on this matter. -A

Well. At least the message was longer this time. She scowled at the note for a moment, then folded it and slipped it into her purse. When she reached India she was going to give him a proper dressing down.

For too long she'd been doing as she was told. No longer. Ida Quimby had a plan for her life and no promise-breaking brother was going to ruin it.

"Bad news?"

Ida turned to find Nick frowning down at her, a worried crinkle across the bridge of his nose.

"Er, well, not unexpected, you see, but, uh…"

Her mouth had come disconnected from her brain. Had she really just thought of him as Nick? How horribly, inappropriately intimate. She had precious few friends she called by first name, and certainly no men besides her brothers.

Had she been out of society too long? The rules of decorum seemed to be slipping away from her.

"Anyhow," she continued, "the message was what I expected, but annoying nonetheless. I'm quite well, however, and ready to go in to dinner."

His frown didn't change and his fingers curled almost into fists. It seemed her irritability was catching.

Ida forced a smile. "Shall we?"

"I suppose."

"Do take care, Mr. Masterson. I wouldn't wish you to injure yourself in all your rampant enthusiasm."

He cracked a smile. "I will proceed with the utmost caution. Thank you for your concern." His eyes drifted down to her purse, his smile vanishing. "And while we are speaking of concern, I did promise no questions, but if someone is causing you trouble I'm willing to offer my assistance. I don't wish to see you come to harm."

"It's a family disagreement, nothing more."

"Your family doesn't like you gallivanting off to the continent all on your own? It is a rare thing, for a young, unmarried woman."

"My family cares far more for their own reputation than for mine."

His dark eyebrows arched. Oh, bother. She'd said too much. The last thing she needed to do was to dredge up old grievances. That was all in the past. Her new, independent life was set to begin, and she didn't need that sort of negativity.

"My apologies," Nick said. "I have overstepped my bounds. I didn't mean to pry."

Except he wasn't looking at her as if he didn't mean to pry. He had that piercing gaze fixed on her, and she just knew he would be peppering her with questions had he not given his word. Not that she could blame him. She was dying to ask him any number of things.

"Not to worry," she assured him. "It was kindly meant. Let's enjoy a nice dinner and speak of cheerier topics."

He pulled out a chair for her, then took his place across the table. "A sound notion. I will leave the choice of topics to you. You are a far better talker than I."

"Well, I can hardly help it. I have four older brothers, and I grew up surrounded by noise."

Nick grinned at her and his eyebrows twitched. Here she went again, violating her own rule and talking about her past. This was harmless, though.

"In order to make myself heard, I had to speak loudly and often," she continued. "I also talked to myself when no one would talk to me. As I grew older and the house grew quieter, I learned that I found silence unsettling. And I like to express my opinions of the world around me, in the hopes someone might listen."

"I'm listening."

"Yes, but you don't always. I've spied that look in your eyes when your mind wanders. I know it well."

"Guilty as charged. Sometimes it's nice to simply let the musical sound of your voice become a soothing backdrop. I do, however, enjoy hearing your opinions, and hope that you continue to express them."

A bashful flush began to creep over her face. Fortunately, before she could open her mouth and stammer some embarrassed thanks for the compliment, a waiter approached and set two glasses on the table.

"Potions to cleanse your palate, mademoiselle and monsieur."

Nick sprang back so forcefully that he nearly toppled his chair. "Take them away!"

"Monsieur?"

"Now. Get rid of them."

"Oui. Of course, monsieur." The flustered waiter snatched up the potions and hurried off.

Nick had gone pale, but he adjusted his chair and squared his shoulders as if nothing unusual had occurred.

"Mr. Masterson? Was something wrong with those potions? I hope they weren't dangerous or anything like that."

"No, no." He cleared his throat. "Uh, sometimes restaurants offer free potions before the meal that bolster the appetite or make you crave more drink. It increases their sales, but the customer may well regret it the next morning if they have overindulged." He didn't meet her eyes. He was lying, but why? What was in those potions, and how had he known without even a sniff or a taste?

Curiosity about who he was and what business he had in Paris once again began to gnaw at her. He had called himself a potions specialist, but she hadn't seen him drink a single one. The only supposed business he had conducted had been when he disappeared for a time at the music hall. Had he gone out after seeing her home last night? His odd, late-night habits did make her suspect him to be a criminal. A jewel thief, perhaps. Or a professional gambler? He seemed clever enough to have a talent for cards. The idea of it gave her a rebellious thrill. She had made friends with a proper scoundrel.

"You're awfully quiet, Berries. I'm sorry if I startled you."

"Why do you call me that?"

He leaned closer. "Because you smell like berries."

"Not today."

"No. Today you smell like vanilla and cinnamon, and it makes me…" He sat back abruptly. "Never mind."

"Makes you hungry?"

Molten-gold eyes fixated on her face. A long, silent moment passed before he spoke. "Yes. Very much so."

Ida shivered. He wasn't the only one. Hunger for a taste of the forbidden swirled inside her. His powerful stare sent hot and cold tingles all up and down her arms. She snatched up her menu to hide her reddening cheeks.

"Have you any suggestions for dinner, Mr. Masterson?

Your knowledge of French food far surpasses mine, and I was quite pleased with your choices at luncheon today."

He studied his own card. "I would suggest either the *caille au gratin* or the *filet aux truffes*, depending on whether you are in the mood for beef or fowl."

"Perhaps we can each order one and then share."

Was that done? It probably wasn't done and she was committing a terrible faux pas. Though considering she was already out, unchaperoned, with a man who was all but a stranger, it didn't much matter whether her table manners were up to snuff. Besides, she was already ruined. The scandal was what had ultimately led her here.

"An excellent idea. And a bottle of Château Larose."

Ida blinked. Château Larose was a pricey wine, if she remembered her *Baedeker's* correctly. Seven or eight francs a bottle. Nick must have done well at the card table last night.

The food and the wine both proved excellent, and she chatted happily as the alcohol eased some of the tension over her coming departure. Perhaps this wasn't the end, after all. They had both come from London. They might meet there, someday. She could find a gaming hall that allowed women and maybe he would come by one night.

A giggle welled in her throat. She may have been a bit more mellow than was proper for a young lady, but it would have been terribly uncivilized to let good wine go to waste. When the gilded clock on the wall chimed seven, she didn't hesitate to down the remainder of her glass.

She pushed back her chair and rose to her feet. A slight rush of dizziness assailed her, but her feet remained steady, and she didn't teeter.

"I'm terribly sorry, Mr. Masterson, but I must depart. Thank you for the excellent dinner."

"Depart?" He came around the table and took hold of her elbow. He had very strong hands. Strong and warm. It was a shame she had to leave him. "Have you evening plans? Did you intend to take in another show tonight?"

"Oh, no. My time in Paris is finished. I suppose I neglected to mention it earlier, but my train leaves at eight p.m. sharp."

He started. "Eight p.m. tonight? You are joking."

"No, indeed. It's an overnight. I have a long journey to my next stop."

He said a rude word and then apologized. "Please permit me to escort you to the cloakroom to retrieve your things."

"Of course."

They headed for the lobby, the movement clearing her head a bit. Her steps slowed. In moments, she would walk out the door, and their time together would be over. Would she ever see him again? Would she learn the answers to the burning questions inside her?

One question in particular plagued her. She had promised to leave the past in the past, but the urge to seize a last enduring memory made her want to go back on her word.

They came to a stop at the end of the hall, just outside the lobby. Nick looked down at her, his amber eyes wide and questioning.

"You are quiet again, Berries. Tell me what you are thinking."

"I… Well…" There was nothing to be done for it. She had to ask. "I'm terribly sorry, but before I go, I must ask you one thing."

The puzzled crinkle appeared between his eyes. "Ask away."

"Are you married?"

He blinked at her. "Am I what?"

"Married. Wedded. Espoused. United in Holy Matrimony."

"I know what the word means."

"Well?"

"No. I'm not."

"Oh." An exhalation of relief passed her lips. "Thank goodness."

She rose up on her tiptoes and kissed him.

VII

Change of Plans

MISS STRAWBERRIES SMELLED LIKE VANILLA and cinnamon and tasted like fine Bordeaux. Nick clutched her to his chest, groaning into the sudden, stupefying kiss. He ran his tongue across her bottom lip, and she opened for him, allowing him free plunder of her sweet mouth, driving him out of his head with her own rapacious explorations.

God, but she was delicious. She clung to his lapels as if drowning, swept up in whatever madness this was that had overtaken them. It had rendered him powerless, and all he could do was hold her and taste her and pray it would last forever. He could lose himself in her perfect, soft lips and her warm, womanly curves, and never regret it.

She broke the spell, sinking back down and loosening her grip.

"Nick," she gasped.

His breaths came hard and fast, his heart pounding out a steady rhythm beneath his ribcage. "Damnation, Berries. That was…"

She lifted a single finger and trailed it over her lips, red and swollen from their passionate embrace. "Marvelous. I won't forget it." She stepped from his arms, her absence leaving a dull ache in the center of his chest.

"Nor I."

She continued to retreat. "I'm sorry we didn't have a longer time together. I will forever be grateful for your friendship. My days here in Paris were everything I had hoped and more. Thank you."

Nick reached for her, opening his mouth to speak before realizing he still didn't know her real name. Goddamn it all, she was going to leave him and he would have no way of finding her.

"I'm very sorry that I must leave, but I can't risk missing the train. Goodbye, Mr. Masterson. I wish you could come with me." She darted in, gave him a quick peck on the cheek, and then whirled away.

Nick stared after her, his brain still half mush from her kisses. She was leaving. Truly leaving.

No.

He had to go after her. Never mind that he had a meeting tomorrow with some English expatriate his uncle knew. He wasn't ready for this to be over. Who would distract him from his worries and problems? Who would keep him so busy that he hardly had time to even think about potions? And, damn, did he crave her kisses now.

Nick ran the three blocks to his own hotel, skidding to a halt and only narrowly missing a collision with the front desk. "Have my trunk taken to the train station immediately, to await me at the ticketing booth."

The stunned concierge flinched at Nick's fierce tone. "At once, my lord."

"Thank you." Nick dumped a few extra coins onto the desk to compensate for the troubles, then spun and jogged for the door. He hailed the first cab he saw, digging his notebook out of his pocket to find the address he needed.

This Lord Westfield lived between the hotel and the train station. Perfect. Nick would spare the man five minutes and no more. He hopped into the cab, offering double the fee for a quick journey.

Westfield's home was a stately old townhouse, grand, but not flashy. Nick took the front stairs two at a time and hammered his fist on the solid oak door.

A craggy-faced butler cracked it open, just as Nick was raising his hand to knock again.

"Ah, someone is home," he sighed in relief. He presented his card. "Lord Sharpe here to see Lord Westfield on urgent business."

The butler frowned down at the card, and Nick stuck his foot in the door to prevent the man from turning him away.

"We have a meeting arranged for tomorrow, but I have been called away on urgent business and must speak with him tonight. I will take no more than five minutes of his time."

The butler reluctantly opened the door. "Please wait here in the hall."

Nick stepped inside and paced the atrium while the butler ambled off altogether too slowly to find his employer.

Nick flipped open his pocket watch. Not enough time. He couldn't afford to be kept waiting. A minute ticked by. Then another. He had just decided to abandon this task altogether, when a middle-aged man in a smartly tailored suit stepped into the hall.

"Lord Sharpe. You wished to see me?"

"Oh, you." Now that Nick saw the man, he recalled who he was. Lord Make-Believe. A self-styled diplomat with a fake title to bolster his reputation on the continent. His life's goal was improving international relations, which made him a useful contact for Lord Ayleston and his band of spies.

"You are Ayleston's nephew, are you not?"

"Yes, I am. I apologize for forgetting our acquaintance. And for missing our prearranged meeting. I'm afraid that an urgent matter has arisen that is taking me out of Paris this very evening. I have only a few minutes to spare."

If that. He would talk fast, pass on his information and ask his questions. No more.

"I hope the matter is not too dire," Westfield replied, a worried expression narrowing his dark eyes. "I don't like this tendency of you young men to rush into danger and I wish your uncle did not encourage it."

Nick huffed a little laugh. "I'm not rushing into danger, I'm merely pressed for time. It's not a matter of life and death."

Except that life might not be worth living without her in it.

Shit. Where had that thought come from? He'd known her for three days. Three. He'd witnessed cricket matches longer than that.

"But as to why I have come here," Nick continued. "My uncle suggested I consult with you regarding the situation with potions here in Paris and in France in general. You have some potions background, I understand, as well as a wide and varied network of friends?"

"I do. I apprenticed with a chemist as a boy. Never took to it, really, but I remember something of it."

"Enough to give me your perspective on the potency of potions about town?"

"They have been weakening in the past few months, if that is what you are getting at."

"It is. The products I have investigated in the past two days seem weaker than I recall from my previous visits. Have you any idea of the cause?"

"I've been looking into that. The serum supply looks to be low. My friend Batista in Spain has reported similar issues. Neither of us has discovered the reasons behind the dwindling supply. The suppliers run the same number of deliveries, there is simply less in each shipment."

"And the price? Is it a set price per delivery, regardless of how much serum is provided, or is it priced by dram or ounce?"

"That I don't know. I will look into it. Can you tell me a little of the situation in Britain? Is it much the same there, also?"

"Yes, from what I have seen and what my uncle tells me. Gladstone suggested he investigate."

"So the Prime Minister is involved. And the rest of Parliament?"

"Many of us know, I suspect, but the matter hasn't been discussed. If the situation is deemed a danger to the empire, I am to present my findings and a proposal for rectifying the situation." He couldn't keep the grimace out of his voice. Lack of serum could cause an economic crisis, and while he was prepared to speak about that, he had no notion how to fix it. If the world's serum was drying up, then alternatives would be needed, but he was no scientist, inventor, or chemist.

At least with no serum there would be nothing tempting him to drink. The grim thought almost made him laugh.

Westfield stroked his moustache. "If something is choking off the source, then the obstruction can be found and removed."

"Indeed. I'm to make my way to India to determine if that is the case."

"But if the source is drying up, alternative sources will need to be found."

"Yes." *If such things exist.* "I hear the Americans have one, but I doubt they have enough to supply themselves and all of Europe." Nick flipped open his pocket watch. "Excuse me. I ought to be going."

"Please, do not let me keep you. You will be sailing out of Brindisi?"

"Yes. I plan to investigate the potions situation in Italy as I pass through."

"Detour to Rome, if you are able. My old friend, George Ainsworth, now the Marchese di Murlo, lives just outside the city. He will have charts, numbers, and statistics for you, rather than my vague words. Ayleston can arrange a meeting,

I'm certain. In the meantime, I will be seeking local potions experts. In the event that we do need to search out new sources, we need the talents of a master."

Nick pocketed his watch and donned his hat. "Try the Folies Bergère."

Westfield frowned. "Pardon?"

"Trust me." He nodded and hurried out the door.

Despite the cab waiting in the street, Nick arrived at the train station just shy of quarter to eight. He ran to the main ticket counter, where a bored porter stood with his trunk. Nick offered up a prayer of thanks and swore to patronize the same hotel whenever he came to Paris.

"What train leaves at eight p.m.?" he asked the man behind the counter. "An overnight."

"Ah…"

"Hurry, man. There cannot be all that many."

The man shuffled some papers. "The sleeper to Turin? By way of Lyons and Modane?"

Yes. That had to be it. "Book me all the way through." He didn't care where she was headed. He'd hop off wherever she did. He tossed money on the counter, not caring that it was probably too much.

"One moment, please."

More paper shuffled. Nick fidgeted with his watch and rocked from one foot to the other. "What platform?"

"Ah…"

Goddammit, why did this man have to do everything so slowly?

"Ah… seven, monsieur."

Nick whirled around to face the porter. "Take my things to platform seven immediately and see that they are loaded." He handed the man one of his few remaining coins and turned back to the ticket counter. "Well?"

More papers rustled, and the man finally passed Nick a ticket. "Here you are, monsieur. One ticket to Turin."

Nick snatched the paper and ran. His heart pounded as he tore through the station, dodging other passengers in his desperate search for the signs that would point him to platform seven. He caromed into a woman carrying a birdcage, causing the creature to let out a painful shriek.

"My apologies!" he called in English. Realizing she might not have understood him, he shouted the same thing in French, not looking back or slowing his furious pace.

Surely everyone thought him a maniac. He was *acting* like a maniac. Perhaps he was one.

His heart leapt at the sight of the train, motionless alongside the platform. He wasn't too late. He couldn't say whether the same was true for his luggage, but for the moment, he didn't care. He vaulted up onto the first car and ducked inside, leaning against the nearest seat to catch his breath.

No sign of her here. He moved on to the next car, ignoring the murmurs over his labored breathing and disheveled appearance.

She wasn't in the second car, either, or the third. By the fourth, panic set in. This wasn't a crowded train. Empty seats were scattered all about. Had she taken some other train? Was there another eight p.m. sleeper to Germany or Spain, perhaps? Nick pushed his way through another set of doors, refusing to accept the possibility. She was here. She had to be here.

At the far end of the sixth carriage, he caught a flash of pink silk. All the tension drained out of him.

My sweet Berries.

She sat with her back to him, and he approached quietly, stopping just behind her shoulder.

"Excuse me, miss?"

Her head jerked around, her jaw dropping open. "Nick! Er... Mr. Masterson. You are on this train?"

"Apparently."

She was still gaping at him. Shit. Had he scared her? He hadn't meant to scare her. Her shock faded into a dazzling smile and his knees nearly gave out. She was pleased to see him. Thank God.

He gestured at the place opposite her. "Is this seat…"

"Comfortable?"

Nick laughed and sank onto the soft upholstery. All was right with his world.

VIII

Bump in the Night

IDA TEETERED JUST AT THE EDGE of sleep when a thunderous, gravelly snort from across the compartment jerked her fully alert.

"Oh, not again," she moaned.

The train was luxurious. Fine food and drink, plush upholstery, lavish decor. Comfortable and beautiful. Everything one would hope for from first class accommodations. Everything except a car free from some sort of snoring beast. After hours listening to croaks and snuffles and snorts, Ida had reached the conclusion that the perpetrator couldn't possibly be human. No man or woman could be so monstrously *loud*.

The snorer shifted or rolled over, or whatever it was that quieted them, and fell silent once more. Ida could only hope that this break would last long enough for her to fall into a deep slumber.

At least Mr. Masterson had fallen asleep. When she had turned in, he'd taken himself off somewhere, not returning until hours later. Since then he'd been tossing and turning, the creaks and groans of the fold-down bunk above her making her fear he might break something during all his shuffling about and come crashing down on her.

Ida giggled into her pillow, the half-hysterical laugh of someone who had passed beyond tired into a hazy delirium. Oh, the look on his face when she had expressed that very concern to him as they observed the conversion of the seating area into beds for the night.

"I don't weigh that much!" he had protested.

"More than average. You are tall and quite, well, substantial."

"I believe these bunks are rather substantial as well."

"It's clear, though, that they weren't designed for a man of your stature. You will need to scrunch your legs up to fit. As for your, er, bulk, I would hope that the beds have been engineered to bear a substantial amount more weight than they are ever expected to hold. A responsible company would have conducted stress tests on all the brackets, especially the connections with the train wall, which is carrying the full load of the bunk and its contents. Or do you think the privacy panels that rise from the backs of the seats are at all load-bearing? That could help distribute some of the weight. Regardless, all the hinges appear sturdy, and the welding is superior from what I can see. The hardware up top is too high up for me to observe closely."

His eyebrows rose. "You've studied engineering."

"Not formally. My father is an engineer. I paid attention."

"Of course you did. Well, I can tell you that the upper bunks appear quite sound."

"To your untrained eye."

He leaned closer, his warm breath tickling her ear. "Are you afraid to have me on top of you, Berries?"

Ida shivered at the memory. Yes. She absolutely was. Terrified, in fact. Because truth was, she expected she might enjoy the experience altogether too much.

When she had kissed him, it had been with the belief that she would never see him again. She had snatched one wild moment of freedom and desire. The kiss had set fire to her veins and unleashed a torrent of lust that could never again be shut away, and still she had been safe. Nothing more could come of it. It would remain only a brief burst of passion with the stranger from the train.

Until that dark baritone had spoken in her ear and she had looked up into those fiery eyes.

All evening she had relived the taste of his mouth, the scent of his skin, the strength of his body. There were possessions of some sort stuffed inside his coat, suggesting criminal more than card sharp. Did he carry weapons? Thinking him dangerous only made him more attractive, like a fierce warrior from an epic tale of old. He would slay the dragon, take the fair maiden in his arms, and drug her with hot kisses. Run his hands slowly down her spine, before cupping her buttocks, dragging her tight against his hard body…

The sound of rushing wind yanked her from her fantasy. Ida levered herself up on one elbow, her eyes searching for the sliver of light where her bed curtains gapped.

A moment later, the noise subsided, accompanied by the soft snick of the door latch catching. A tingle of unease crawled up her neck. What purpose could anyone have moving between train cars at this time of night?

Her ears strained to catch the muted footfalls, praying they would come to a halt at the lavatory. The washroom in the next car over was probably out of order, and this passenger had need of the facilities. Her trepidation was no more than her fevered imagination assigning him nefarious intentions.

The careful steps continued on, with no sound of the lavatory door opening. Ida's palms began to sweat. Her breath caught in her throat as the stranger neared her bunk, and the shadow of a figure appeared through the crack in her curtain. The intruder stopped and turned.

Ida shrank back against the wall, her heart threatening to pound its way out of her chest. Her fingers clutched her pillow, prepared to use it as a shield should this man mean her harm. She had no knife, no hatpin, nothing that could serve as a weapon. Even her parasol was packed away with her luggage. Only her own hands and her wits could save her.

The intruder didn't bend down or reach for her curtain, and a new fear tore through her mind. Nick! Was this some creditor come to beat him for unpaid debts? Some hostile competitor upon whose criminal territory Nick had encroached?

Did it even matter? He was asleep. Defenseless. He could be stabbed, poisoned, strangled, and no one would discover the murder until morning. She was his only hope.

She sucked in a deep breath and released her loudest, most ear-splitting scream.

IX

The Night Watch

Nick bolted upright so fast he smashed his head on the ceiling. He shouted an obscenity and dropped to the floor in time to see a dark-clothed man bolting for the carriage door. For an instant, he remained frozen in indecision. The desire to chase down and pummel the villain raged through him. But what if Berries was hurt? What if she needed him?

Her head popped out of the curtains, her face showing no signs of tears nor pain. Nick took off running.

He flew out the door, leaping the gap between the train cars and barging through the door, not caring who he woke or disturbed. His legs were miles ahead of his brain. Who the hell was he chasing? What even had happened?

Berries had screamed, that's all he knew. Berries had screamed and Nick was going to chase down the villain who had frightened her. His prey was nearly a full carriage-length ahead of him, but Nick had a longer stride, and the train was a finite length. He *would* catch the bastard.

If this turned out to be a dream, he was going to feel extraordinarily stupid.

He raced into the dining car, stumbling to a halt just in time to avoid impaling himself on an upended chair. The carriage was in a shambles. The door at the far end slammed closed.

Nick blinked at the disaster for a moment, his mind at last coming fully awake. The villain, whoever he was, was no fool. A few seconds' worth of knocking over chairs and Nick's pursuit had been thwarted.

"Goddammit," he growled, shoving his way through the overturned furniture, his pace slowed to a near crawl.

By the time he stepped into the next car, his quarry had vanished. Nick ran one car further before admitting defeat. The man could have ducked into a bunk, or hidden himself in a lavatory. He was tall and lean, wearing a dark suit. No distinguishing features. Dozens of men would fit that description. He was well and truly gone.

Nick spun and hurried back toward his own bunk, cursing himself for leaving Berries behind unprotected. The cold, hard floor stung his stockinged feet. As he stepped carefully from one car to the next, the magnitude of his recklessness filled him with shame. One little slip in the darkness, and he would have been crushed beneath the wheels of the train.

What had he hoped to accomplish? A dozen brief investigations didn't make him a trained spy or soldier. That man could have had a gun or a knife, or been trained in a deadly martial art. Nick hadn't even remembered to arm himself. His defensive potions sat crammed in the corner of his bunk, unused and unguarded. He'd reacted out of anger and run off on a dangerous, foolish whim, leaving the woman he'd promised to protect alone without so much as a word.

He pushed open the door to their carriage, prepared to admit his failure to apprehend the miscreant and apologize for not seeing to her needs.

"How dare you, sir?"

Nick staggered to a halt. There she stood, with her back to

him and hands on her hips, staring down an older gentleman while curious neighbors peered out from their bunks.

"I have already explained the reasons for the disturbance," she continued, "and while I dislike that it had to happen, I won't apologize for it. You have no right to put your own desire to sleep above the safety of every person aboard this vehicle. I scared off a suspicious and potentially dangerous intruder, and to imply that I would have been better served to leave him to do harm is appallingly selfish and patronizing."

Nick stepped up behind her, letting his hand brush against hers. "Trouble, my sweet?"

She whirled and threw her arms around him. "Nick! I was so worried! Did you catch him?"

"I'm afraid not. But never mind that. How are you?"

"I'm well, thank you."

"That's more than the rest of us can say!" the irritable man snarled. "Wakening the entire car with your hysterical screams."

"Her screams weren't near as bad as your snoring," a woman's voice called from behind a curtain.

"That's not the half of it," the man continued. "Refusing me an apology. Stomping up and down the aisle in nothing but a nightgown. Tormenting respectable people with her shameless behavior."

"Shut your mouth," Nick commanded in his deepest, most lordly voice. "You will apologize to my wife and return to your bed. Now."

She stiffened in his arms. He would beg her pardon for the lie once they were off this blasted train. For now, it seemed the best way to safeguard her reputation, given their mutual state of undress and the way she had flung herself at him. He hugged her protectively to his chest and glared at Sir Snores-A-Lot until he took himself back to bed in a huff. He hadn't apologized, but he wouldn't be bothering her anymore.

Nick sat down on her bunk and pulled her down to sit

beside him, holding her hand in silence while their fellow passengers closed curtains and returned to their places for the remainder of the night. When the noise died down, he slid all the way into her bed, propping himself up against the wall and drawing her into his lap. She settled herself comfortably, her head falling back onto his chest. Nick rubbed a lock of golden hair between his thumb and forefinger.

"Tell me what happened," he whispered.

"That man entered our carriage and came to stand before our beds, facing you. Having had a bit of time to think on it, it's possible he was searching for something. In the moment, all I could think was that he meant you harm. So I screamed."

"Thank you for your concern and your quick thinking. I'm relieved to hear he didn't attack you in any way."

"No, indeed. I'm certain he was here for you. Have you done something illegal? Angered the wrong sort of person?"

"Not that I'm aware of."

Nick bit his lower lip, contemplating her words. He couldn't recall doing anything out-of-the-ordinary. He had nothing of particular value with him, he had no real enemies he knew of, and he could think of no reason for anyone to follow him on a mere fact-finding mission. He had assumed the man had been after her, thinking her unprotected and perhaps in possession of money or jewels.

If only Nick hadn't bungled the chase. Now they would never know the villain's true purpose.

"I know you carry something concealed in your coat. Weapons? Valuables? Something that might be worth stealing?"

"Potions." He didn't elaborate, not wishing to dwell on the various items that made up his travel kit. Too many of them were drinkable, and the cravings had been gnawing at him since drinking Elle's potent concoction. And then there was the little toy he kept perpetually in his trunk or in his left, front pocket. Difficult to explain.

She interpreted his silence as displeasure with her. "I'm so sorry, I shouldn't pry. We promised no questions."

"A decision I have come to regret. Perhaps in the morning we might reevaluate the situation."

"Yes, perhaps." She yawned, her body sagging against his. Nick tugged the bedding up and over her.

"Sleep, Berries. I will keep you safe."

"Yes, but..." Another yawn. "Who will keep *you* safe?"

He pressed a kiss into her hair. "Who indeed."

Ruffians aside, he felt safe here, holding her close, breathing in her subtle, sweet perfume, basking in the warmth of their entwined bodies. He toyed with her hair while she drifted off to sleep in his embrace.

He would wait up the remainder of the night, acting the concerned husband he had claimed to be. Never mind that they had only just met and he still didn't know her real name. He would be her guardian, the way she had been his. And while he drew breath he would allow no harm to come to her.

X

Revelations

IDA'S CARPETBAG LANDED atop Nick's trunk with a dull thud. She beamed at the young porter who had carried it down from the train so promptly.

"Thank you so much…" She looked for his name badge. "Jean. You have been a wonderful help. And I'm so terribly sorry for all the chaos last night. I hope you didn't receive too many complaints."

"Only a few, *madame*."

Ida's gaze flicked to her curmudgeonly antagonist, who was berating a different porter because his luggage hadn't yet appeared. She hoped it would be the last trunk off the train.

"Goodbye, Sir Snores-A-Lot," she whispered.

"And good riddance," Nick added. He winked at her and tossed Jean an extra coin.

The porter tipped his cap. "Merci, monsieur, madame. Enjoy Italy."

Nick offered Ida his arm. "Come, darling, let me take you to dinner before we go to our hotel. I'm famished, and I haven't had a proper pesto in at least a year."

She tried not to squirm as she took hold of his arm. Being addressed as "madame" was peculiar enough, but when he called her "darling" and played the gallant husband it turned her into a nervous ninny. He was so darn good at it, and she was the blushing mess who would give them away. The farce needed to end before she landed them both in trouble.

The moment they were out of sight of anyone who might think of her as Mrs. Masterson, she released him, putting a bit of distance between them.

"I think it's time to be done with this charade, don't you?"

Nick slowed his pace, turning to frown down at her. "Not if it means you will run away from me. Come here, Berries. We can hardly have a private conversation while you are five feet away."

Ida swatted his arm. "If I were five feet away, I couldn't do that, now could I? And I'm not running away. I'm being practical. I made arrangements under my own name. I can't simply arrive at the hotel with a husband in tow."

Nick slid closer, eyebrows twitching mischievously. "We could be newlyweds. We had a romantic elopement to Paris, and now we are on our honeymoon."

"Strange, then, that I would have arranged rooms and tickets for just one."

He took hold of her hand, lifting it to his lips. The soft pressure against her gloved hand made her belly tighten and brought an unexpected smile to her face. She knew she ought to be pulling away, but the laughter in his eyes warmed her inside and she let herself linger in the pleasure.

"I see how it is," he sighed. "Less than twenty-four hours as my wife and already you wish to be rid of me. It's another man, isn't it? Not that snoring fellow, I hope."

Ida couldn't smother her laugh. "You have uncovered my secret love! Alas, our sham marriage is doomed!" She slapped the back of her hand to her forehead in a mock swoon. "Woe is me."

Nick flung an arm around her, as if to support her during her fainting spell. "Sir Snores-A-Lot would have no patience for a vaporous wife. Admit it, darling, you are better off with me."

"Well… I suppose you do know all the good food, and I am a bit peckish."

In truth, her brief stint as Mrs. Masterson had been nothing but delightful. She had slept soundly in his arms, as though she belonged there, safe and warm in his embrace. After a morning bursting with questions about their nighttime adventure, the remainder of the day had passed quietly. Nick had spent much of the time dozing, his feet propped up on the seat next to her and his hat pulled down over his eyes. Ida read her *Baedeker's Italy*, jotted notes for a few new perfumes, and had several pleasant chats with fellow passengers. More than one woman had remarked on how lucky she was to have such a dashing and devoted husband.

He will make a wonderful husband, but not for you, she reminded herself. They would part ways soon. Eventually. Their matching itineraries couldn't continue on indefinitely.

Nick chose a cozy restaurant not far from her hotel. He procured them a secluded table in the corner, read the menus, and placed orders for them both.

"I ought to have brought a little phrasebook," Ida said. "I'm glad your Italian is so good."

"Actually, my Italian is rather terrible. I'm sure I pronounced half my words wrong or got the grammar all scrambled up. But I do know most of the words for the food. I ordered us both the pesto. You will enjoy it."

"And while we wait, perhaps we can have that talk about whether to discuss more of our pasts and futures."

"I vote 'yes.'"

"It is unanimous, then," she said, "as I also vote 'yes.'"

"Excellent. What would you like to know?"

Everything. "I suppose the sensible place to begin is to ask where you came from and where you are going."

"I came from London, as you know, and I'm going to India."

Ida jumped. "You are?" No wonder they had followed the same path. Would he follow her same schedule the entire way? A little thrill raced through her at the thought. "I, too, am bound for India. How remarkable. What is your business there?"

"I'm looking into a matter for my uncle. Asking questions and seeking information. More than that, I'm not permitted to say."

"Not permitted? But why… Oh! Are you a spy?"

"You could say so, though it seems an exaggeration of my actual tasks and abilities. I talk to people and make observations. No adopting disguises or sneaking about or that sort of nonsense. My uncle's professional spies get paid for their work. I get reminded of my duty to my family."

"I thought perhaps you were a criminal or a gambler. On account of your odd hours and vague business."

The corner of his mouth twitched upward. "And I thought you were fleeing an arranged marriage. Or running off to elope with a lover your family disapproved of."

"My family couldn't be roused to the effort of arranging a marriage for me any longer. And they would never disapprove of anyone who wished to marry me. The neighbor's footman could propose, and they'd be thrilled to have me off their hands."

"That makes no sense. You are a lovely, intelligent, self-possessed woman. How could anyone possibly think of you as either unmarriageable or a burden?"

"I caused a scandal and ruined an important business deal," she admitted.

Not that any of it had been her fault. Her teeth clenched and her blood boiled thinking about it. Even now, two years later, it still made her furious. She would never get over the injustice of it all.

His jaw tightened. "I see."

His amber eyes had hardened, and she wondered what he might be thinking. Would he think less of her, as so many had done? Would he demand to know more? If he moved in loftier circles, he would have known already. It had been the talk of the town, to hear her parents tell it.

"You deserve far better than a footman," he said at last, his voice a soft growl that sent shivers across every last inch of her skin. "An earl at the least."

Her anxiety melted away, replaced by a massive blush at his bold praise. "You flatter very nicely, Mr. Masterson, but I never pretended to have such lofty marriage goals, even before the incident."

"I see." Another long, awkward silence fell, but before she could fill it, he asked, "What, then, is your purpose in traveling to India, if not to escape or procure a husband?"

"I'm seeking serum."

He flinched. His claim not to be a proper spy wasn't modesty. She had upset him, somehow, with that statement, and his emotions were plain to see in his expression. A professional would bluff better.

"What for?"

"For my business. You know all the perfumes I wear are of my own creation."

He nodded.

"I have been working for the past two years to build a product and a customer base. I produce custom scents for ladies of quality based on private consultations. But to win over the elite clientele, I must have something truly unique. To that end, my final goal is to incorporate potion-based perfumes. I wish to make perfumes that maintain their scent for certain lengths of time, perfumes that change, that mask particular odors, and things of that nature. I have developed prototypes, but I can't produce them in quantity without a steady supply of serum. My supplier hasn't fulfilled his end of our agreement. Therefore, I'm going to him to demand answers and take my first shipment back home with me."

Nick leaned back in his chair, folding his arms across his chest and regarding her with a satisfied smile. "You, my dear, are a remarkable woman. I applaud your ingenuity and your tenacity, though I'm sorry that you have had to apply them so diligently. Whatever you may have done in the past, your family shouldn't have been so unfeeling as to force you to provide for yourself."

"Oh, they provide for me well enough. I have a comfortable home and an allowance to provide for my needs. But I prefer to make my own way. Once my business is successful, I will be free to leave and I will no longer have to be the girl no one wants."

He leaned forward abruptly, desire shimmering in his eyes. "You will *never* be the girl no one wants."

Ida's breath quickened, her heart pounding in her chest. She fought the urge to lean across the table and kiss him. What on earth had come over her lately? Were France and Italy really so romantic that her natural passions were all aflame? Or was it simply him?

The waiter appeared with a bottle of wine before she could give in to any foolish impulses, and they settled into a relaxed conversation about Italy, Italian food, and whether the wine was better here or in France. She argued for France, and Nick for Italy, but they both agreed that a proper Scotch whisky was better than either.

"And why does a young lady such as yourself even drink whisky?" he asked with a chuckle.

"I told you, I have four older brothers! I wasn't going to be left out of sneaking into Papa's liquor cabinet."

He toasted her with his wine glass. "To you, Berries.

A woman worthy of the loftiest of goals, be they marriage, business, or otherwise."

She lifted her own glass. "To the sweetest flatterer in England."

"I speak only the truth." He downed his drink, then rose from his seat and walked around to pull her chair out for her. "Shall we head to the hotel? I would like to see you settled safely in your room, in case any more suspicious strangers come prowling about."

"The suspicious stranger was after you. You are the spy."

"I've done nothing but ask a few harmless questions. It makes no sense to come after me."

"It makes less sense to come after me."

"That is no reason not to be cautious. I need to go out tonight and ask more harmless questions, but I will make certain you are safe before I do so."

"And what of *your* safety?"

He patted his coat. "This time I will have my defenses with me."

Ida made a little huff of displeasure, but didn't argue. Really, what right did she have to tell him how to conduct his business? One glorious kiss and a beautiful night snuggled together didn't give her any claim to him. Just because he looked at her as if she were the only woman in the world—as if he truly saw and admired *her* and not merely who she was supposed to be…

Oh, who was she kidding? Something had sparked between them during this journey. She didn't know where it was going or whether she ought to be going along with it, but it was undeniable, and she knew he felt it too. So she would worry and fuss and try to keep him safe, whether she had a right to or not.

They walked to the hotel in relative silence, Ida making only a remark or two about the city, while her brain mulled over arguments for why he oughtn't go out alone.

"I will see to our luggage," he said when they arrived. "And send a separate bellhop with your bag so you needn't pretend to be my wife any longer."

She nodded. *We are not a couple. This is temporary. Remember that.*

The concierge at the desk smiled as she walked up. "Hello. I am Miss Ida Quimby. You have a room for me for one night?"

He checked his book. "*Si, signorina.*" He fetched a key for her while she signed the guestbook. "And I have a message for you as well."

"A message?" But Alfred had said he wouldn't write again. She shook her head. It was just like him to say one thing and then do another.

Nick walked over just as she was unfolding the note. "Your luggage is in good hands and ready..." He stopped when she turned toward him. "I beg your pardon. Please, finish your telegram."

"Oh, I won't be but a moment." Her eyes dropped to the paper, curious what sort of complaint her brother had this time.

She gasped, her eyes scanning the words in disbelief. Her hand trembled.

Nick sprang to her side. "What? What's wrong?"

Ida held out the note to him. "I... I..." She took a deep breath. Her words came out in a whisper. "But why would anyone want me dead?"

XI

New Arrangements

Proceed further and your life *is forfeit.*

Nick crushed the paper in his fist. The need to defend her raged through him with the same wild intensity it had last night on the train. He didn't know why she triggered such protective ferocity in him, but the longer he knew her, the more it seemed to grow. Today, with no enemy at hand, he could do nothing but stand there, shaking in impotent fury. He couldn't even embrace her to comfort her in such a public location.

He spun toward the desk. "Is the room next to hers available?"

"One moment." The concierge turned away to check his records, shaking his head. He fetched two keys and slid them toward Nick. "I can put you in these two rooms, if you wish to be side-by-side. The view is better, however, so the price will be higher."

"I'll cover the difference for the lady's room," Nick replied, before she could object.

She traded keys without protest and he scrawled something in the guestbook without even looking.

"Upstairs. We need to talk."

She only nodded.

By the time they reached the rooms, Nick had calmed down enough to begin assessing the situation rationally. It made no sense. He could see no reason anyone would wish to do her harm. Unless she had lied about everything and was some sort of spy or criminal herself. If so, he was the biggest fool to ever walk the earth, because he was prepared to help her in any way he could.

"In here." He ushered her into his room and flicked on the nearest lamp. The pleasant, potion-fueled light illuminated what had to be the ugliest hotel room he had ever had the misfortune to lay eyes upon. "Good God."

Her fingers clenched on his arm. "What?"

"This room looks like it was decorated by an undertaker."

"Oh. It is a bit stark, I suppose."

"The bed looks like a tomb, I'm certain those curtains were once a widow's best mourning gown, and the wallpaper… well, the less said about that, the better. Also, with the way the furniture is arranged, the place is practically unusable."

"I see."

"That, at least, I can do something about. I'll fix the furniture. You talk."

This would be perfect. It would help keep his head clear. He grabbed the small writing desk and dragged it to the center of the room to make space for the washstand that belonged in its place.

"So, this note of yours. 'Proceed further and your life is forfeit,' it said. I assume such death threats are a rarity."

"This is my first, as far as I know." She possessed remarkable poise, under the circumstances. No fainting, no weeping. Not even any trembling, now that the initial shock had worn off. She simply stared at him as he rearranged the room.

"Do you know of anyone who might wish you harm?"

"No."

"Who have you been communicating with on this journey? That serum supplier?"

"Yes."

"Would he threaten you, do you think?"

"Certainly not! He's my brother. He will yell at me plenty, but he would never wish me dead!"

"Could it be his idea of a joke, then?"

"No. He wouldn't do that. If it were Francis, perhaps, but Alfred is much too serious. He isn't likely to joke at all with me and certainly not about something like this."

Nick tilted the massive wardrobe and kicked an accent rug underneath to allow for easy sliding. "All right, then. Someone else."

"Let me help you with that." She put her hands against the wardrobe to steady it as he dragged it across the room into its new position.

"Thank you. Now, there must be a reason for someone to threaten you. What have you done?"

Her whole body went rigid. "What have I done? What have *I done*? Nothing! I have done absolutely nothing, and how dare you—"

"Whoa. I'm sorry, I'm sorry," Nick interrupted. "I didn't mean…" He took a deep breath and tried again. "I don't believe you've done something wrong. What sorts of things have you done recently that might, say, draw negative attention, or upset someone? A rival perhaps? Do you know any angry perfumers who are jealous of your business? Will your potion perfumes catapult you to stardom and leave someone else a distant memory?"

"Don't be ridiculous, Mr. Masterson. Perfumery isn't literally a cutthroat business. Where do you want this rug?"

"Over there, where the new sitting area will be. Let me move that armchair first."

"It seems clear that the message was meant to scare me off.

Someone doesn't want me to continue my journey to India. But I can't imagine what anyone would gain from stopping me."

"Your brother would benefit from it, because then he could avoid telling you he doesn't have any serum for you."

"What do you mean? How would you know that?"

Nick sat down in the armchair and surveyed the room. A few tweaks remained, but it was vastly improved. He hopped back up and went to adjust the desk.

"Serum supplies are running low. At home in England and also in France. I will be verifying that the same holds true here in Italy, and, ultimately, I'm headed to India to determine the cause of the problem."

One blond eyebrow rose. "I thought you weren't allowed to tell me what you were investigating."

"I told you I wasn't a very good spy."

That got a smile out of her. "Not a professional."

"No."

"What *is* your profession, Mr. Masterson?"

Landowner. Peer. Seat in the bloody House of Lords.

For a moment, he considered revealing his full identity. Would she take it in stride, the way she did so many things? Or would a lifetime of social indoctrination skew her view of him? His gut twisted at the thought of her curtsying and addressing him as "my lord."

He answered instead with a wave of his hand, displaying his newly rearranged chamber. "This. Residential design."

For a moment, she stared at him with that too-familiar look that said he was crazy. The 'earls don't move furniture' look. A smile quickly replaced it, and she glanced around the room, studying his handiwork.

"You do seem to have a knack for it, but I don't think it's a real profession."

"It is now. And the transformation would be much better if I could also redo the tapestries and the lighting and especially that wallpaper."

"It does look a bit like, well, dirt."

"You are being generous. I was thinking horse shit."

She laughed, then covered it with a cough. "There is no need for crude language, Mr. Masterson."

"There is every need. You can see it as well as I. I shudder to think what your room might look like."

Perfect pink lips tilted in a flirtatious smile. "Why don't we go take a look?" A blush followed a few seconds later. Nick's entire body tightened. He was certain she had only realized after she spoke how suggestive her offer was. And yet she didn't take it back or stammer an awkward clarification. Her eyes remained fixed on his, her smile still coy, with a hint of shyness. "I don't mind if you come in for a moment."

Or an hour. Or all night.

Forget her room. They were already alone, and he wanted her. Wanted to toss her onto that unsightly bed and rip the pink dress from her body. He would bet that her corset was pink, too, and her drawers. He would take his time removing those. Exposing luscious pink nipples, and then lower to…

Bloody hell.

"I should be going," he said. Or growled, more accurately. It was either sound irritable or sound aroused, and he preferred to chase her off. Otherwise she might kiss him again, and then God help him. "I have more questions to ask tonight. You should turn in for the night. You will be safe with the door locked."

She folded her arms across her chest and gave him a pouty frown that made her lower lip plump out. "And what about you? How will you stay safe?"

"I'm not the one receiving threatening messages and being stalked by strange men in the night."

"The strange man was after you."

"I think not. I think he was there to give you a fright, just like the telegram. Someone thinks he can scare you off."

"Someone doesn't know me. I mean to see this through.

First thing in the morning, I'm getting on the train bound for Brindisi."

Nick flinched. "Like hell you are."

"Excuse me?"

"You are not getting on that train. Not alone. You're coming with me to Rome."

"That isn't my itinerary. I have tickets reserved and a steamer to catch. I won't alter my plans for you or for anyone."

"You could be in danger."

"I'm not afraid of bullies."

"Look," Nick pleaded. "I'm not asking you not to go. I'm only asking that you don't go alone. I have a meeting scheduled in Rome. It will only be two days, and we can see the sights, like we did in Paris."

Sadness gleamed in her blue eyes. "I'm certain that would be lovely, but my future depends on this mission. I don't have the funds required to rebook everything. It was all planned in advance."

"I know it was. You're the most organized person I've ever met in my life. Don't you ever do anything spontaneous?"

She strode to the door and opened it, and for a moment he thought she would walk away without another word. But then she paused, her hand still on the doorknob, and glanced back at him.

"I kissed you, didn't I?"

Nick took a step toward her. "Berries."

"Goodbye, Mr. Masterson. I'm so sorry our travel plans don't match any longer."

She hurried away, leaving nothing behind but the sorrowful thunk of a closing door.

XII

Crime and Punishment

THE NEXT MORNING, Ida gently closed the door to her hideous hotel room with its poorly arranged furniture. Her gaze slid to the next door over. It would be hours yet before Nick woke. If he was even there. She hadn't heard him come back from his late-night spying.

She took a step toward his room. Perhaps she could merely verify that he had returned safely.

Stop it, Ida. It's not your concern. He has his job, and you have yours.

This was worse, somehow, than when she'd thought they were parting ways in Paris. Then she had kissed him, and departed clinging to a special memory. This time they had quarreled, and she wanted nothing more than to barge into his room and create some new memory to erase the awkward goodbye of the night before.

Trains, though, didn't wait, and she had an itinerary to follow. She handed her bag over to a bellhop and headed down to the lobby to settle her bill and hail a cab.

Outside, the damp chill of the predawn air seeped through

the layers of her pink traveling dress, and she tugged her coat tightly closed. The small clouds of her breath drifted silently skyward, shimmering in the lamplight.

The lights here were gas, not potion, she noticed. Was it true, what Nick had said? Was serum running out? The merchants she had spoken with back home had said nothing of the sort, but their quoted prices had been exorbitant. Enough that buying from them would mean selling her perfumes at a far greater price than she had planned. And while one of her goals was to sell to the highest ranks of the aristocracy and the most fashionable ladies of London, she couldn't begin there. Nor could she depend on people notorious for hopping from one fad to another. She needed a solid customer base of women of her own social circle—or what once had been her own. Wives of wealthy tradesmen, daughters of knights and baronets, women of the upper middle class who aspired to more. They would be her first and best customers. And to woo them she needed affordable prices.

Alfred had promised her top quality serum below standard cost. With his position as a valued employee of the Imperial Potions Company, it had seemed a reasonable claim.

He lied to you.

She'd been trying not to think it. Not to believe it. She would never have been so confident in his claims in the first place if Papa hadn't raved about what a good job Alfred had found and how he would be advancing in the company in no time.

Her father had no reason to lie, that she could see. It wasn't as if Alfred were the embarrassment of the family. Ida had sole claim to that title.

Her maudlin musings occupied her for the duration of the ride to the train station, a fact which didn't bode well for the fifteen-hour journey to Brindisi. Every moment she expected the brush of a hand against her arm, a tall presence beside her, or the glint of warm, amber eyes meeting her own. He would be grumpy this early in the morning, answering questions with terse, grunted words and downing pots of black coffee.

Stop, she scolded herself. She could make a new friend on this train. Nicholas Masterson was hardly the only agreeable person in the world.

Ida reached for her bag, prepared to carry it until she could find a porter with a cart to wheel it to the train. Her fingers had just curled around the handle, when a gloved hand shot out and wrenched the bag from her grasp.

She gasped and stumbled, confusion slowing her reactions and giving the thief several seconds' head start.

"Moldwarp!" Ida blurted, her Shakespearean curse word giving her less satisfaction than she desired. She hiked up her skirts and took off running.

"Stop! Thief!" A few heads turned, but no one moved to help her. "*Au voleur!*" The pounding of her heart matched that of her boots along the pavement. "Oh, how do you say, 'stop that man' in Italian?"

Even with the burden of her heavy bag, the thief pulled further away with every step. The slim, fashionable skirts of her dress prevented her from taking full strides, even when yanked scandalously up to her knees. It was a beautiful dress, one she adored and had imagined herself twirling around in to show off to Nick. If only she had done so yesterday and had been more practical today, instead.

"Stop!" she cried again, in a last, desperate effort to save her belongings.

Much to her shock, the thief did just that. He skittered to a halt, glancing back in her direction. Then he tossed her bag into a nearby carriage and clambered in after it.

"No!" Ida hiked her skirt up higher, no longer caring if all of Italy thought her a harlot. "You… you… maggot licker!"

She reached the carriage in time to see the villain disappear out the opposite door. Her bag, miraculously, lay abandoned on the floor.

"Oh, thank God," she gasped, stepping up into the vehicle and dropping her skirts.

Both doors slammed at once. The carriage lurched, sending her sprawling across the seats.

"No, wait, stop!" She yanked her parasol from the bag and rapped it on the roof. "Stop this carriage!"

Either the driver didn't hear her or he didn't care, because the carriage shot off down the street as if an army of marauders was hot on their heels.

Ida braced herself against the door, staring out the window at the buildings flying by. Did she dare try to jump? At this speed, a fall onto the rough ground was certain to cause injury. Could she use her luggage to break her fall? Or perhaps execute a dramatic tumble, like one of those acrobats she had seen at the Folies Bergère?

Not in this dress.

She pounded on the roof again. "Stop this carriage at once! Stop, I tell you!"

The vehicle careened around a corner, tossing her onto her rump. Another turn quickly followed. She pounded more, shouted more, but when several minutes passed with no response, she was forced to admit defeat. Even if the carriage were to stop, she would be hopelessly lost, in an unfamiliar city where she didn't speak the language. She had no chance of making it back to the station in time to catch her train.

"Oh, balderdash," she grumbled, not even having the energy to come up with something creative.

Tears blurred her vision. She had worked so hard, planned so carefully. All to have her future destroyed by some unknown enemy. For some purpose she couldn't fathom. She had no rivals among the perfumers she had met in London. Her potion plans were known only to a few. She meant to be a relatively small, selective business, so no industry giant ought to be threatened by her plans. Who would wish to stop her so badly? Who would wish to ruin her? She dabbed at her eyes with a handkerchief and let herself mourn.

A little tremble of fear shook her. Was that awful note serious? Did this mysterious kidnapper truly mean her harm? She squared her shoulders. Whoever they were, they wouldn't find her weak or biddable. She would fight for her life. She would fight for her business. Her enemies would rue the day they decided to deprive an innocent woman of her life's work.

Another quarter hour passed, by Ida's watch, before the carriage stopped, allowing her plenty of time to gather herself and prepare to face down her kidnappers. The door opened, and a red-faced driver held out a hand to help her down. Ida grabbed her bag and climbed out unassisted.

"*Mi dispiace, signorina.* Sorry. You are well?"

Ida only glared at him. "Where am I?"

A deep voice spoke behind her. "Only just outside town."

She whirled around. "Nick! What are you..." The question died on her lips, the guilty look in his eyes all the answer she needed. "*You* did this!"

"I'm so sorry, Berries."

Sorry. What a useless, worthless *nothing* of a word. Sorry wasn't good enough. Sorry couldn't restore her future. Sorry couldn't begin to soothe the rage and the pain of his betrayal.

She stalked toward him, burning with righteous anger, her cheeks flaming and her muscles clenching. "You!"

He didn't flinch away from her fury, merely clasped his hands behind his back, awaiting his fate with sorrowful eyes.

"You horrid, awful..." Words failed her. She grasped for something more. Something to convey the true depth of her outrage. "Bloody arse!"

Ida swallowed back her shock at her own crude words and slapped him hard across the face.

XIII

Too Quiet

IF SOMEONE HAD TOLD HIM on that chilly morning in Turin that a man could die from silence, Nick would have scoffed. Now, two days later, he would merely nod and agree, because she was ripping his heart out, bit by agonizing bit, all without so much as a word.

He deserved it, of course. He'd been so terrified of what might happen to her that he'd latched on to the first solution that sprang to mind, never thinking *he* might be the one terrifying *her*. He hated that he might have done just that. And even though he'd altered her plans, he would never destroy her life's work. He would see her all the way to India, as she desired.

But safely. Out of sight of any enemies. Her safety was worth the price. He'd seen no suspicious persons since deviating from her intended course, and she'd received no messages, threatening or otherwise. If he had to go back, he would do the same thing all over again. Even if she never forgave him.

Berries danced down the street, reenacting some ancient Roman battle or festival, or whatever it was the Colosseum had sparked in her imagination. He didn't know. She wouldn't reveal her thoughts to him. She seized joy wherever she went, but unlike in Paris she would share none of it with him.

He led the way to the restaurant she had picked from her guidebook, pretending not to care and knowing she saw right through him. They reached the door at the same moment as another couple, all four of them halting to avoid crowding the entrance.

"Excuse me," the other woman said.

"Oh, you speak English!" Berries answered with a smile.

"Yes, we are American. Come, we must share a table!"

Nick started to shake his head, but Berries nodded enthusiastically, grinning at everyone except him. He grimaced and flipped open his pocket watch, using his old habits to distract from the hitch in his breath every time she turned away from him.

Four days, sixteen hours, nine minutes.

It felt longer. Paris seemed a lifetime ago. Turin nearly so. He'd stumbled upon a wild crowd of potion drinkers there and nearly relapsed again. Thoughts of her had sustained him. Worry for her. He hadn't slept that night, too busy making the arrangements to prevent her from getting on that train.

Selfish bastard. You did this to keep her close as much as to protect her.

He snapped the watch closed.

Three days, seventeen hours since we kissed. Two days, five hours since she last spoke to me.

He ran a finger absently across his cheek. The sting of her slap had long since faded, but he would welcome it back in a heartbeat, just to feel her touch on his skin.

"It's always such a pleasure to meet a fellow English speaker," gushed the American woman.

"Indeed," agreed the man with her. "We are Mr. and Mrs. Holbeck from Delaware. And you are?"

He looked straight at Nick.

"Uh…" Damnation! He still didn't know Berries' real name. How in hell was he supposed to introduce her? "I'm, uh, Nick Masterson, and, er…"

"I'm Miss Masterson. His sister," she said, before he could do anything idiotic, like introducing her as his wife again. Though that's how they were registered at the hotel. He wasn't going to let anyone treat her with disrespect for traveling alone with a man. He'd forced her into the situation, therefore it was his responsibility to see that no harm came to her because of it.

"Lovely to meet you," the American woman replied. "Have you been in Rome long?"

"We arrived only last night from Florence," Berries answered.

"Oh, Florence is so lovely! I hope you were able to see some of the sights."

"I was. The Gallerie degli Uffizi were amazing, and the Duomo is more fantastically beautiful than I had ever imagined."

And yet it had paled in comparison with the golden-haired beauty standing beside it. Nick remembered every detail. The wonder shining in her blue eyes. The way she twirled in her pink dress, laughing at how she matched the bits of pink marble in the facade. Her sweet mouth, opening to say something to him in her excitement, then snapping abruptly closed, telling him more than any words could that he had no right to her friendship.

"Oh, and I was able to see the Venus on the Half-Shell painting in person," she continued, leading their party to a nearby table. "I mean Botticelli's *Birth of Venus*, of course. She's standing on half a shell, like some oyster, so that's what we called it. My brothers used to giggle over the reproduction in our art book because she was naked. It was terribly silly, but I thought it a beautiful painting, and I'm so happy to have seen it."

"…Eh, Masterson?"

Nick glowered. He'd been enjoying the enthusiastic recounting of their sightseeing, content to pretend she was talking to him. Damn Mr. Hol-Whatever from Somewhere in America and his disruptive conversation. Not knowing what the question was, Nick made a noncommittal grunt, hoping that the snub-nosed American would interpret it as he liked.

"Women do prattle on," Snub-Nose said with a shake of his head.

Nick put the full weight of his aristocratic upbringing behind his condescending scowl. "I rather like it."

Berries lifted her eyes to his, and for an instant the world narrowed to the two of them, nothing more than this shared look and the ghost of a smile on her lips.

She glanced away, severing the connection. He would need more than a few kind words to earn her forgiveness. He would need to give her the world. If only he knew what bits of the world she wanted.

"Will you be in Rome long?" Mrs. Snub-Nose asked.

"Oh, no," Berries replied. "We set out for Brindisi after lunch tomorrow. We will see the sights today and a bit in the morning, assuming I can drag Mr. Masterson out of bed at a reasonable time."

"You have dragged me out of bed every day this week." He couldn't remember the last time he'd had a proper night's sleep.

"Do you know people with morning difficulties, Mrs. Holbeck?" she continued, as if he weren't there. "I don't understand it, myself. I can't sleep at all once the sun begins to rise, so I may as well get up and begin the day, don't you think?"

"And she does this without the benefit of coffee," Nick added.

She ignored him, turning the conversation to the merits and hazards of train travel.

Tease me, he pleaded silently. *Poke fun at me. Scream at me. Slap me again. Anything.*

"Dashed fine wine they have in this country, don't you think?" Snub-Nose drawled.

Nick checked his watch.

Four days, sixteen hours, nineteen minutes.

Berries joined him on his visit to the Marchese di Murlo, out of curiosity more than anything, he suspected. She didn't say, of course. Nick could see the stiffness in her shoulders and her fidgety movements as she struggled not to say anything to him that wasn't strictly necessary. His punishment was no easy task for her, yet she persisted. He admired her tenacity. Which only exacerbated his own anguish.

"Westfield didn't mention you would bring a friend." The marquess gestured at the chairs in front of his massive desk. "Please, have a seat."

"She's his wife according to the hotel logbook."

Nick jumped, his head swiveling to locate the unexpected voice. In a corner of the room, a young man perused a bookshelf, his black-clad figure obscured by the shadows.

"Henry, stop skulking," the marquess said.

"I enjoy skulking. Did you wish to know the young lady's real name, or shall we pretend she is Mrs. Masterson?"

Please, God, tell me her name. I swear to recite it over and over until I remember.

"I'm Nick's sister, Miss Masterson, today," she said primly. Nick stifled a groan. "Now, I understand you have some sort of report? What can you tell us? Is serum really running out?"

And just like that, he found himself left out of his own conversation. Berries and the marquess reviewed price comparisons, delivery reports, testimonies from local merchants and consumers—about a dozen papers in all. He let them talk, having nothing in particular to contribute.

The numbers validated his observations. Potions were weakening and serum supplies dwindling. This was just what he needed to make his report to Parliament. Half his task was done. Tomorrow he would set out for India to determine whether he could identify a reason for the problem. And get Berries back on her desired path, though now with first class accommodations and no more trouble from her mysterious enemy.

Murlo rose from his seat. "Well, this has been an excellent conversation. Please give my regards to Ayleston and let me know if you learn anything further. I'm still holding out hope that the situation is only temporary and order will soon be restored." He helped Berries up from her seat, clasping her hand in his. "It has been wonderful to meet you, Miss Masterson."

She smiled back at him. "It was a pleasure, my lord."

"The pleasure was all mine, I assure you." He looked down at her in a contemplative way, tossing a glance at his skulking son.

Nick's whole body tensed. If the marquess thought to make a match between Berries and that short, blond, freckle-faced…

Skulker stared down into his book, pretending not to notice. Not interested. Good. Nick didn't want to have to fight for her. He wasn't particularly good at fisticuffs, to be perfectly honest. He preferred a battle of wits. Or, better yet, a battle of aesthetics.

He gestured at the door. "Let's be on our way, Berries. I'd like to show you more of the city."

She glanced up at him, and again he felt that split-second connection before she looked away. He wasn't sure how much more of this he could take.

"Yes, I have many sights to see and little time to see them, I'm afraid," she told Murlo. "We must take our leave of you. Thank you for your help. We will be in touch."

"*We* will be in touch?" Nick echoed once they were alone. "Have you gone and made yourself part of my mission, then?"

"You forced me to it. If you didn't want me participating,

perhaps you should have considered that before you kidnapped me."

Nick found himself smiling. That was the longest sentence she'd said to him in two and a half days. "I'm happy to have your participation."

"Hmph."

"What would you like to see next? The Pantheon, perhaps?"

She popped open her reticule and handed him a slip of paper. "Here is the itinerary."

She ran him ragged for the remainder of the day, but Nick preferred it that way. The busier she kept him, the less he dwelt on his troubles. And as much as it smarted when she ignored him, he still managed to absorb some of her delight at seeing a new part of the world. He returned to the hotel with a bit more hope than he had left with that morning.

Nick walked her up to their adjoining rooms—with a connecting door that may as well have been a wall—thinking to see her safely locked in for the night before going out on his own for a bit. Ten p.m. was far too early for him to sleep.

He rounded the corner and stopped short. A man lounged against the wall beside his door. Putting himself in front of Berries to shield her from possible harm, he continued on, reaching into his coat for a nasty potion to spray on the man, if necessary.

The man turned and Nick relaxed. Lord What's-His-Face's skulking son.

"Newlyweds with separate bedchambers?" The young man shook his head in mock sorrow. "How tragic."

Berries sniffed. "Traitorous husbands don't deserve the company of a loving wife."

Her frosty smile speared Nick right through the chest. He hated that he had hurt her. Despised it. Despised himself. But he didn't know what else he could have done.

"What do you want, Freckles?" he snapped, venting his

anger on the inoffensive man. "Does your father have more papers for us or are you merely being a pest?"

"I thought you might wish to know you are being followed."

Nick blinked. "Followed? By whom?" He thought back over their day, but could recall nothing suspicious. They'd doubtless encountered some of the same people at multiple sights, but no one stuck out in his memory.

"Man of average height and build. Dark brown hair, light eyes, possibly blue or gray. Hard, square jaw. Snub nose."

Berries gasped. "The American?"

"He's not an American. The accent is fake."

"Who is he, then?" Nick demanded.

Freckles shrugged. "No idea. But I thought you should know. Take care." He nodded to them. "Sharpe. Miss Qui... Masterson."

Qui... Nick's brain groped for the distant memory. *Quigley? Quincy? No. What was it?*

"Nick." Berries clutched his arm, but the distress in her voice ruined any pleasure he might have taken in her touch. "I... I told them all our travel plans."

He cursed. So much for keeping her safe.

XIV

Setting Sail

"'Persons troubled with sea sickness should choose a berth as near the middle of the ship as possible.' Hmm. Well, we can ask to change rooms, I imagine. I'm certain the crew will understand."

Nick only grunted.

Ida glanced at the steamship docked nearby, sitting deceptively still in the quiet water of the harbor. Soon enough it would be bouncing across the Mediterranean, and Nick would be only too happy to trade his situation for an early morning on dry land. Unless she could convince him to try some of the cures in her guidebook. She looked back down at the text.

"Oh, dear."

"What?"

Ida read the next line. "'Aperient medicine taken the day before will often prevent an attack.' I'm afraid it's too late for that."

"Good. I don't fancy spending half a day on the toilet."

Ida's eyes darted back and forth, looking to see if anyone had heard him. "Nicholas Masterson, that is…"

"True?"

"Appallingly inappropriate to speak of in a civilized conversation."

"You brought up the matter, and it's far too early to be civilized."

"It's half past eight."

"And you woke me an hour ago and I haven't had a single sip of coffee or the smallest bite of breakfast."

"Oh, but that's for the best. Your stomach needs to be cleansed and relaxed at the time of departure."

"Rubbish."

Ida glanced away to hide her smile. Really, she ought not to take pleasure in his surliness, but this new punishment was such an improvement. Not speaking to him had been effective, but it had driven her so mad that she'd gone and spilled far too much information to random strangers at a restaurant, and possibly put them both in danger.

Playing tour guide gave her plenty to talk about, provided him with useful advice, and maintained a certain distance in their relationship.

A sadly necessary distance. Her anger, frustratingly, had done nothing to diminish her attraction to him. His voice still warmed her insides. The heat in his amber eyes made her shiver. Too often she reminisced about their kiss and the night spent dozing in his arms. The worst of it was, as arrogantly high-handed as his behavior had been, she knew he had done it out of genuine concern for her wellbeing. He cared for her, and he was doing all he could to make her delayed passage to India comfortable and safe.

She despaired of maintaining an appropriate measure of fury under such trying circumstances.

If only he would admit he had been wrong. That he should have given consideration to her thoughts and her feelings. That she was an adult, competent and capable of making her own choices whether he agreed with them or not. Then she could forgive him. They could talk things out and he could atone for his mistake.

But he was stubborn.

Well, she could be, too. She returned to her book.

"Three drops of creosote in a little water half-an-hour before embarkation, and repeated every half-hour on a piece of sugar, is an excellent palliative," she read.

"That sounds revolting, and regardless, I haven't any creosote."

"Nor have I, but I did procure some ginger root. You should try it. The book also says, 'Medicinal potions to relieve symptoms of the sickness for longer duration are often available onboard for purchase by first class travelers.'"

His brows drew together. "No potions."

"No? But it seems the best option. Effective and long-lasting. Is the price a concern? I can make arrangements to pay a portion…"

"I will not drink potions."

She flinched at the harsh tone of his words. "I don't understand. Why can't you drink them?"

"I *can* drink them. I will not."

"You carry potions on your person but you don't drink them?"

"Correct."

"Even if they could be of help to you?"

"Even then." He flipped his watch open and stared at it for a moment, then snapped it closed without a word.

"I see. Or, rather, I don't. How can you call yourself a potions specialist without drinking any potions?"

He gave a bark of harsh laughter. "Perhaps I'm better termed a recovering potions specialist."

Understanding dawned. "Oh! A bad experience with recreational potions? My father hosts parties of that sort, and I understand such things happen from time to time."

"The experiences were always what I desired them to be. But they were all too frequent."

"Ah. I'm sorry." Was that even the right thing to say? Ida

fought a blush, embarrassed to have driven him to admit to his weakness.

Nick turned to stare out at the shimmering waters of the Mediterranean, clasping his hands behind his back. "Addiction is a funny thing. I've know people who indulge frequently and don't suffer for it. Among the less fortunate, some men crave only the effects of the potions. Others hunger for the very serum that gives them their potency."

"What did you crave?"

"Both. And 'do,' not 'did.' It doesn't go away. It merely becomes… manageable. More or less. There are good days and bad."

Ida made a thorough study of the back of his coat. She had no words to offer him. Nothing seemed adequate comfort and she feared to tread on his vulnerability.

"You help."

Her mouth dropped open in shock. "P-pardon?"

"The pleasant timbre of your voice. The different scents you wear each day, as unique and interesting as yourself. The way you smile and laugh at every new sight. Your relentlessly positive outlook. You brighten every day. You make me remember that there is joy in the world."

"Nick." Her hand settled on his arm before she could think better of it.

He whirled around and their bodies collided. All the air went out of her lungs. His head bent toward hers.

She ought to have taken a step back. Turned away. Anything but tilting her lips upward in invitation.

His lips brushed over hers, sending sparks skittering across her skin. His hand lifted to cup her face, his thumb grazing her cheek in a silken caress.

"Strawberries again today," he murmured. "Like the day we met."

And then his mouth claimed hers, kissing with such desperate hunger that she could do no more than cling to him and let herself be swept up in the madness. He was drowning, and she had jumped in after him, not knowing whether she would save him or merely be washed away with him.

"Berries. God." He pulled her tighter against him, pressing kisses along her jaw and nipping gently on her earlobe.

Ida let out an incoherent groan. Her entire body was afire. Her fingers dug into the wool of his jacket, steadying herself as the world swayed beneath her. She kissed whatever part of him she could reach—his glistening lips, his stubbled jaw, the exposed skin of his neck, where his pulse beat rapidly in time with her own. He was all fire and passion and strength.

"Berries," he moaned again.

She sucked at the sensitive skin of his throat. "Say my real name."

He stiffened and took a step back, his hands falling away from her. "Goddamn." He swiped a hand through his hair, undoing the half-hearted attempt he had made to tame it. "What am I doing?"

Ida's chest heaved. She could still feel the scratch of his unshaven jaw against her lips. His musky scent filled her nostrils. Her legs wobbled as if she were already at sea.

The world drifted slowly back into focus. Nick's words filtered into her brain. What *were* they doing? And in public, no less. Even married couples were not so... demonstrative.

She widened the space between them, gathering herself. As the passion of the moment subsided, anger flooded in to take its place. Anger at him, for putting her in this situation in the first place, but also at herself for forgetting that he wasn't to be trusted.

She smoothed out her skirts and regarded him with what she hoped to be cool detachment.

"You forget yourself, Mr. Masterson. We aren't friends."

"No."

The single, husky syllable vibrated in her chest, the weight of his inflection speaking for him.

I want you. I crave you. We aren't friends. We are more.

Ida turned away, retrieving the guidebook that had slipped to the ground during their embrace. "It appears boarding has begun. I will see that you get some ginger root and that our cabins are in a suitable location."

"As the lady desires."

He needed to stop talking. Every word melted her insides. Why had she been so foolish as to kiss him again?

"I desire you not to be seasick for the entire journey."

"Your concern is appreciated."

Ida strode toward the ship. This wasn't working. She needed to stop talking to him again. Clearly she couldn't control herself otherwise.

She joined the crush of other passengers, focusing on looking for the fake American couple who had joined them for lunch in Rome. Nick hovered behind her, his looming presence both a comfort and an irritant.

"I have seen no sign of the Fauxmericans thus far," he murmured.

"Nor have I. Hopefully they have failed to follow us here and you aren't in any danger."

"Why do you insist that they are after me?"

"Because you are a spy, even if an amateur one."

"But the threatening message came to you."

She waved a hand in dismissal. "Probably from my brother, angry I wouldn't heed him. Besides, we are traveling *your* path now. Someone rather rudely interrupted mine, if you recall. Someone who seems to think he has the right to decide my life for me."

She didn't need to look to know that he was cringing. "I don't have the right... I'm sorry."

"So you've said. Enjoy your voyage, Mr. Masterson. I'll send you the seasickness remedy." She lifted her skirts and hurried off.

A short while later, she reached their adjoining cabins,

near enough to the middle of the ship that she didn't think changing rooms would be of any benefit. Nick had followed her the entire way, but he hadn't tried to say anything further, and she had neither looked at nor spoken to him. She unlocked her door and slipped inside, leaving him to his own devices.

Like the first class hotel rooms they had occupied in Rome, her cabin was lit by a potion-fueled lamp, mounted on the wall near the door. She turned the light up brighter and froze in shock.

The handle of a knife jutted straight up from her pillow. She skirted around the bed, not taking her eyes off the weapon. Another warning. This time from a villain who had been in her very bedchamber.

A villain who might still be in the room. She flung open the closet door, half expecting some ruffian to spring out at her, but the cupboard was empty. No one lurked under the bed, either, and the small chamber contained no other possible hiding places. She was safe, for the time being.

Ida pulled the knife from the pillow and examined it. A simple steak knife, probably stolen from a kitchen. She tucked it beneath the edge of her mattress, where she would have easy access to it in the event of an intruder. Whoever her stalker was, he wouldn't find her a cowering, helpless miss. She checked the lock on her door, then wedged the chair from the dressing table beneath the handle.

"Hugger-mugger," she cursed, plopping onto the bed. Nick was right. Someone was after her. Whether to scare her away or do her real harm, she didn't know, but she couldn't go on pretending that everything was normal. She would have to take steps to protect herself.

Her eyes fell on the connecting door that led to Nick's bedchamber. She pushed herself up off the bed, strode over, and unlocked it.

XV

Right and Wrong

DAMN. SHE WAS RIGHT.

Nick leaned against the rail, feigning illness and angling the hand mirror to get a glimpse of the man who had been watching him. Not the Fauxmerican. Tall and lean. Thin faced. It was impossible to tell for certain whether he was the midnight intruder from the train—especially considering Nick's sleep-muddled memories—but the man's height and build were the same.

Muttering another curse, Nick slipped the mirror into his coat pocket. His fingers brushed a slim syringe, loaded now with a potion that could render a man unconscious within seconds. A defensive measure he had taken to protect *her*. And yet it seemed she had been right all along. After three days in a confined space, he could no longer deny it. Thin-Face, whoever he was, was after him.

"Mr. Masterson, are you ill again?" Berries rushed toward him, her blue eyes all wide concern. "You ought to be lying down. I'll fetch you the ginger root. I knew you shouldn't have drunk all that coffee this morning."

"It wasn't the coffee," he growled.

She shook her head at his surly reply. "You needn't pretend for me. There is nothing shameful about seasickness. It's a scientific fact that it often affects even the most virile of men."

Her cheeks turned a delightful shade of pink, giving Nick the sudden urge to demonstrate just how virile he could be. He pushed the thought away. Time enough for that sort of thing later, when he could be certain they were out of danger. And assuming she ever forgave him.

"Come, you must at least sit," she insisted.

"I'm not…" He stopped himself before he could begin an argument. The fake illness had been his own damn idea, and he needed to maintain the role as long as anyone might be watching him.

Truthfully, he hadn't been seasick since the first, miserable day. Well, except for a brief bout when a squall had caused rough seas for a few hours. But for most of the voyage he had felt entirely himself.

He'd spent much of that time wandering the deck, scowling at anyone he thought might pose a threat to Berries. She, meanwhile, buried her nose in her guidebooks, rarely speaking to him except to impart some new piece of medical advice. Much to his displeasure, the entire ship now believed him an invalid.

He turned and gripped her wrist just above her lacy pink glove, the skin-to-skin touch sending an electric sizzle up his arm. His scowl deepened. Damned inconvenient time for both his mind and his body to become overstimulated. Not that amorous thoughts were ever far from his mind when she was near.

"Perhaps a brief sit-down," he said.

He took a single, staggering step and she immediately threw an arm around him. He sagged against her with just enough of his weight to put on a convincing show. His eyes swept the deck, but Thin-Face had vanished into the crowd.

"Honestly, I don't know what you were thinking," she

scolded, sounding for all the world like a nagging wife. Nick scowled more to hide a threatening smile. "Three days of this, and still you insist upon pushing yourself."

He bent his head to hers, his lips nearly brushing her earlobe. "I'm not ill, but keep playing that I am."

Her arm tightened around him, but she otherwise showed no surprise.

"You are the most vexing man, Nick Masterson."

"A thousand apologies, my lady, for heaping undeserved troubles upon you." His tone was lighthearted, but his sense of remorse was anything but. He'd recklessly snatched her from her intended course, angering her, frightening her, and throwing all her plans into disarray, and for what? To expose her to even more danger? He was such an ass.

"I'm not a lady, as you well know," she replied, doing a masterful job of hauling him across the deck, despite their size imbalance.

No. You are Miss Qui–

Quick? Quillian? Quimet? And what the devil was her given name?

"A lady would have servants to drag her afflicted husband to his bed and tend to his seasickness." Her eyes drifted up and down his body. "And to tidy him up before he went out in public."

Nick grimaced. Was she referring to his unshaven jaw, his old coat, or his lack of a necktie? Perhaps all three. He hadn't given much thought to his casual appearance and lack of servants. During these investigations for his uncle he preferred to look the part of a middle-class businessman or a dissolute layabout, as circumstances dictated. Now, though, the itch of stubble on his face reminded him that Berries didn't fully know who he was. Another thing he had to be sorry for.

The moment they descended below deck, she abandoned the pretense of assisting him, putting distance between them rather than taking his arm as a true wife might do. Given what he was about to confess, she might never touch him again. Why hadn't he savored it while he had the chance?

He unlocked the door to his cabin and ushered her inside. "Please, sit."

She glanced around the room a moment, then perched on the edge of the bed, settling her skirts comfortably around her. She had donned his favorite dress again, the pink with black stripes. The same dress she'd worn the day he kidnapped her.

He sank onto the too-small dressing table chair, biting back a growl of frustration. Well past time to get this over with.

"I owe you a monumental apology."

One golden eyebrow lifted. "I believe that is a well-established fact," she said. "I admit that paying to rebook all of my transportation and accommodations has aided your cause in some *small* part. And I did greatly enjoy seeing the sights of Florence and Rome. However, don't think that means that I will simply…"

Nick held up a hand to stop her. "Please. I do not expect or deserve your forgiveness, but I must speak. I was wrong. Obviously. I destroyed something important to you, something that you had put a great deal of work into. I forced you to go with me against your will. At the time I believed it the only thing to do, but looking back… It was appalling, inappropriate, and condescending. Behavior of the worst sort, which ought to be beneath any decent man. You have my deepest apologies for being anything but decent.

"But it's worse than you know. Not only was I wrong in what I did, but I also erred in my reasoning for doing so. You have been right all along. That man on the train was after me. He is after me still. He is here, on this very ship."

"What?" She went rigid. "You are certain?"

"As certain as I can be. I never got a close look at him on the train, but this man is of similar stature and has been spying on me since we came on board."

"How did you discover that?"

"As you know, the first day I spent almost entirely in my room, but the second day I felt well enough to venture out for breakfast."

"Yes, I remember. I warned against the coffee and the bacon. You ought to have heeded my advice."

"My illness later that day was due to the storm, not to anything I had eaten. And it is irrelevant. I didn't notice anything unusual at the time, but by luncheon I had an odd sense that a man in a navy blue jacket seemed to be everywhere I was. I began to look for him."

"Is that why you fought against returning to your room that afternoon, even when you were turning remarkable colors of green?"

"Yes. You and I had been together all day, and I believed he was after you. I feared to leave you unprotected."

She burst out laughing. "For goodness' sake, Nick, you were hardly able to stand on your own two feet! How did you think you could protect me? Vomit on the enemy?"

"I didn't give the matter a great deal of thought."

"An unfortunate habit of yours."

Nick winced. "Guilty as charged. We can't all be planners, my dear. But as I was saying, you know that eventually I did give in and return to my room. I believe you promised to do the same, but when I reemerged several hours later, you didn't respond to my knocking."

"I was in the library, reading up on India, which you would know if you had bothered to ask when you found me. You were so disagreeable that I declined to dine with you."

"I was terrified something had happened to you in my absence!" Nick raked a hand through his hair. "I had it all wrong. I didn't see you again until this morning, but I spied a navy jacket on multiple occasions last evening. Usually at a distance, or just a glimpse of a man in a crowd. He was at dinner, and I even thought I saw him at the end of our hall just as I was returning to my room."

"And today?"

"More of the same. He is wearing gray today, but he's been watching me. I have yet to determine why or what he wants. But it is definitely me and not you. He follows me when we are apart." Nick massaged his temple, trying to alleviate the burgeoning headache. "I can't even explain how sorry I am. I should have listened to you. I know how intelligent you are. I know you have good ideas. But I was too bloody stubborn. And all this time I have been the one in danger, not you."

A peculiar expression crossed her face. Not quite embarrassment, but something like it. She almost seemed ashamed, though he couldn't determine why that might be.

"Nick, I think there is something you should know."

"Of course, darling, in a moment. I will let you say anything you like for as long as you like, but I must get this off my chest. Please believe that everything I did was because I believed you to be in danger. It doesn't right the wrong. It doesn't excuse me. Nothing can. But I want you to know that I would never intentionally do you harm. I never wanted to hurt you or frighten you. But I did. I wounded you. I insulted you. I made a reckless, impulsive decision when I should have stopped and considered your thoughts and your feelings. And the result is that in my misguided attempt to keep you safe, I have involved you in my own troubles. I can never forgive myself. I won't expect you to do so, either."

"Nick. You… you weren't wrong. I am in danger. I think. As much as you are, I would say. I, too, am being followed."

He jerked so hard that his chair teetered precariously. "By the thin-faced man?"

"No. By the Fauxmerican woman. Only once did I get a good look at her, but I'm almost certain she has been shadowing my movements. I haven't seen her husband—if he even is that. But she has trailed us to this ship and will likely continue after us all the way to India." Her shoulders sagged. "So I was right. And you were right. We both have stalkers. I can't fathom why or guess at what they might want or whether they truly mean us harm, but I think it's clear we must both proceed with the utmost caution."

"Bloody hell," Nick muttered.

"Yes."

"Will you agree, then, to stay close to me? There is safety in numbers and I swear to do all I can to protect you." He thought for a moment, then added, "With your permission."

She nodded. "I agree. I will do all I can to protect you, as well. I'm certain you will need me, as you are likely to be ill for the next two weeks and I don't have all that much ginger root."

"Oh, for God's sake, I'm not seasick! It passes after the first day or so."

"Yes, well, it's best to be prepared. We shall dine together tonight, and it might be wise to remain in our rooms until then. Have you locked your door? You can wedge that chair underneath the handle for added security. I know it will upset your aesthetic sensibilities, but these rooms aren't especially beautiful in the first place."

"The paint color is unfortunate, but I will persevere."

"Good. I will try to devise a plan. We can discuss it tomorrow on the train. Until dinner, then." She hopped up from her seat, walked to the connecting door, and opened it.

Nick gaped at her. "When did you unlock that?"

"Nearly the moment we arrived. You know, in case you needed me." She nodded and disappeared into her room. He stared after her, no longer able to make sense of the world that only moments ago had seemed entirely clear.

"Well, damn."

XVI

The Mean Streets

"Don't you have a knapsack or small travel bag for today's journey?" Ida patted her own small satchel. "We shall not see our luggage again for above twelve hours. The guidebook recommends such 'as may be stowed under a railway seat.' I would think you might at least desire to bring a hairbrush and a shaving kit."

Nick only shrugged. He'd been sullen and silent since their talk yesterday. Not that she expected differently. He grew quiet when he was anxious. She babbled, of course.

"Or have you decided to grow a beard?"

He hadn't shaved since Italy. At first she had blamed it on the seasickness, but now she wondered if he were merely being lazy. He would still look handsome with a beard, certainly, but he had such a nice jawline and a particularly fine mouth. It would be a shame to obscure those things with too much facial hair. She had to admit she rather liked him in his current state. The urge to run her hands over his chin and cheeks was near overpowering. Was he still scratchy, or were the hairs just long enough to be fuzzy? How would those short whiskers feel against her skin if she were to kiss him now?

Clearly she wasn't meant to be a Lady. A woman of that class would be expected to prefer her men one way or the other rather than in some vaguely unkempt in-between state. Most people would attribute her preferences to her humble birth. Daughter of a mere tradesman. Aspiring to better than her station. She'd heard it often enough in the days when the Scandal was fresh. Her fall from grace was "to be expected" and "a sign of her common roots," as though she were a lower form of human entirely.

The words hurt, but Ida refused to be cowed by them. She could be just as ladylike as any member of the aristocracy. Where her actions and opinions differed, it was because she refused to make herself into someone else's idea of ideal womanhood. She could dine with the Queen *and* run a profitable business, thank you very much. And she could admire slightly scruffy and peculiar men if she pleased.

"If you have quite finished your scrutiny of my personal appearance, perhaps we might debark?"

Ida sprang back, allowing him passage through the door and glancing away to conceal her blush.

"Not that I mind being admired by a beautiful woman," Nick continued. "But I must warn you, if you make a habit of staring at me, it may be taken as a sign you actually like me. And we wouldn't want that, now would we?"

Oh, dear. The teasing would be the end of her. The slightest smile on his face and her heart turned to goop.

"I do like you, Mr. Masterson. You are grumpy every morning without fail, drink too much coffee, stay up too late, make impulsive decisions, rarely listen to reason, and always think you are right. And yet, somehow you manage to be kind and funny and charming at all the right moments. You are good and caring. Even when I am furious with you, I find myself liking you. Apparently, it can't be helped."

"Are there no suggested remedies in your guidebook to help you dislike men you meet on a train?"

"Sadly, no. And I understand the impudent ones to be the most difficult to rid oneself of."

He grinned at her and when he offered his arm she took it.

"How long before our train departs?"

"Two hours. We should have time to buy a bit of food for the journey. You see, this is what comes of altering the plans. This company doesn't provide refreshments. Now, we must take care with what we purchase. And don't drink the water here. It is brackish. The guide recommends pale ale and ripe oranges."

"Let's find some, then."

For half an hour they walked the streets of Alexandria without finding a single suitable bit of nourishment. Ida led them this way and that, navigating as best she could from the scant information in her *Bradshaw's Guide*. Nick followed her in silence, gallantly refraining from commenting on the failure of her quest.

"Oh, I think if we head back this direction—" She turned and let out a yelp as a man with a knife leapt out from the shadow of a nearby doorway.

Nick whirled around at her cry, letting out a sharp curse when he spied the villain.

Ida flipped her parasol in front of herself like a shield, letting her guidebook tumble to the pavement. "Go away! I haven't any money!"

She jabbed at him with the tip of the parasol, sizing him up as she did so. His features were obscured by a hooded cloak, but the tidiness of his clothes suggested he was no mere cutpurse. The man who had been tailing Nick? Or one who had been tailing her?

"Don't meddle where you don't belong, girlie," the man snarled, slashing with his knife. The blade sliced a long gash in the fabric of her parasol. "You've been warned."

A second man stepped out into the street, chuckling and leering. His hand slipped inside his coat.

Ida's fingers clenched around the handle of her parasol.

The sturdy shaft and stout ribs would keep the knife wielder at a distance, but if this second man had a gun…

Nick flew past her, a bit of metal flashing in his hand, launching himself at the second enemy. The two men crashed together just as the gun appeared, but before the villain could even lift the weapon he toppled over, unconscious. The knife man whipped around and charged.

"Nick, look out!"

Nick spun to meet the attack, raising the small syringe that was his weapon. Ida snapped her parasol closed and swung it at the back of her enemy as he grappled with Nick. The blow hit him square in the kidneys and he staggered. Nick jabbed him with the needle and he joined his companion in a heap on the ground.

"Damnable blackguards, attacking an innocent woman. I ought to…" He swayed on his feet. Their eyes met for an instant, then dropped to the glittering handle jutting from Nick's abdomen. "Oh, fuck."

Ida's parasol clattered to the ground and she seized his arm before he could fall and drive the knife further into his gut.

"'S not bad."

"Sit." She helped him to the ground. "Lie back." She tore open his coat, blinking for a moment at the array of little vials sewn into the lining. "Which ones are healing potions?"

"Won't drink—"

"Which ones!"

"Three on the top left. No, my left." He gritted his teeth. "I'll be fine. Just a few stitches."

"It could get infected. And you could bleed out before we can get you to a surgeon. You need the potion."

He squeezed his eyes closed. "The third one. Can be spread on the wound. Don't let me watch."

She pulled out the little bottle and set it beside her. "First we need to remove the knife so I can assess the damage."

She took care to grasp the handle gently, but even that

slight movement caused him to flinch and cry out in pain. She gave an experimental tug and he screamed and jerked.

"You must lie still."

"Can't. Hurts."

"You'll tear the wound more."

He waved a hand at the syringe he had used on their attackers. "Sleeping potion. A few drops will put me out long enough." Ida retrieved the syringe and pushed up his sleeve enough to poke the needle into his arm. "Not too much. Don't want to leave you…"

She depressed the plunger for only a second and he slumped into unconsciousness. One firm tug freed the knife and started a gush of blood. She peeled back his waistcoat and shirt, mopping up the blood with her handkerchief to allow her to inspect the wound.

Narrow, but deep. Pouring the healing potion over it would heal the surface, but damage and potential infection could remain underneath. She needed to get the potion inside to heal him properly.

Her eyes fell to the syringe. She hopped up and jabbed both of their attackers with it again, expending all the remaining sleeping potion. Then she refilled it with the healing potion. Working as methodically as she dared, she pumped small amounts of potion deep into the wound, edging her way back out until the entire gash had been coated with the pale pink liquid. She spread the last bit over the top of the wound, watching the flesh begin to knit together as the magic took effect.

She exhaled in relief. He would live. The potion would continue to mend the damage, and if he showed any signs of ill health as the day wore on, she would use another on him. Even if she had to pour it down his throat.

"Nick." She gripped his shoulder and shook gently, trying to rouse him. "Nick, can you wake up?"

He didn't so much as twitch. She had no idea how much

of the sleeping potion she'd shot into him, but she couldn't sit around waiting for it to wear off. Not in a strange city where they had already been set upon once.

She made a quick check of their assailants. Neither carried any identifying papers. They looked like local men, but not street criminals. Mercenaries, she suspected. Hired thugs. But hired by whom?

Ida tidied Nick up as best she could, then fetched her damaged parasol and her guidebook. She opened the slim volume and flipped to the page that listed the address of the British consulate. She would drag him there if necessary.

XVII

Sweet Surprise

Nɪᴄᴋ ᴄʟᴜɴɢ ᴛᴏ ᴛʜᴇ ᴅʀᴇᴀᴍ, hating to leave Berries there, sprawled across his bed in delicious dishabille. She shouldn't be alone. He needed to stay with her. To kiss her. To make her moan with pleasure.

The infernal clacking noise tugged him further into consciousness. Why was the room swaying beneath him? Why was his bed so damned small? Where the hell was he?

Nick opened his eyes to stare at the unadorned, cream-colored ceiling. A curved ceiling. And a very narrow room.

He jerked upright. "What happened?"

"Oh! You're awake." Berries hopped up from her seat and crossed the tiny chamber in a single step. "No, don't get up. You've had a rough morning."

"What time is it? How did I get here? And what is all this?" He gestured at the room around him.

"A private train compartment."

"I can see that. But what are we doing here?"

"Traveling to Suez."

"For the love of… I'm not daft, and I didn't take any blows to the head. *Why* are we in a private compartment?"

"I decided you needed a quiet, secluded location to recover. Please, lie back down. You have had an eventful morning."

Nick rose from the bed so that no more than a few inches separated them. "I'm perfectly well. How much of that potion did you use on me?"

"The healing potion? All of it."

"All of it?"

"You had a huge gouge in your side. I worried about bleeding and infection. One can never be too careful. My oldest brother is a physician, so I have heard all about the true causes of infection. You see, there are these microscopic *animalculae* called germs, and if they aren't properly cleaned from the wound…"

Nick gritted his teeth. "I'm familiar with germ theory."

"Ah. Good. Then you understand that I had to be most thorough in application of the medicinal potion."

"That potion cost a fortune." He shook his head. "Well, I suppose I needn't worry about suffering any lasting effects."

She gazed up at him. A touch of red rimmed her ocean-blue eyes. Had she been crying?

"Please lie down. You need to rest."

"I've rested plenty. What time is it and how did you get me onto this train?"

"Well, if you must know, I dragged you to the consulate—with the help of a few friendly locals—where they were understandably upset at an attack upon a British citizen in broad daylight. They were kind enough to help get you onto the train. I paid to upgrade our tickets to the private compartment."

"I will reimburse you."

"No need." A small crinkling around her eyes exposed her lie.

"There is every need. You can't sacrifice your perfume business for me."

"I can do whatever I wish. You risked your life to protect me."

"And you saved it. You owe me nothing. If anything, I owe you, for altering your plans, not believing you, forcing you to do things my way, getting myself stabbed, and leaving you alone to tend me."

"You *were* rather impulsive, rushing to my defense like that." She lifted a hand to his cheek. "And gallant." Moisture glistened in her eyes. "I was so scared, Nick. I didn't even know how much until I got you here and locked the door, and then I just cried and cried."

He brushed away a stray tear with his thumb. "My brave, sweet Berries."

She lifted up on her tiptoes and sealed a kiss to his lips. Nick's arms wrapped around her, tugging her close until her soft breasts crushed against his chest.

Damn, but she could kiss. Her blushes and glimpses of shyness suggested a certain degree of innocence, but when she gave in to her passions there was no holding back. She became scorching heat and desire and eager explorations.

And what better indulgence for a man than her unending sweetness? Far better than drinking. Far, far better than mind-altering potions.

Nick sank down onto the bed, pulling her with him. When she lifted her skirts to settle onto his lap, he let out an inarticulate growl, clutching her waist and dragging her closer to his rapidly stiffening cock. He nuzzled the soft skin of her neck, inhaling the scent of her and the subtle perfume she had dabbed in strategic locations. A hint of cinnamon today.

His gaze traveled down her body, over the swell of her breasts peeking out above her square-cut neckline, all the way to the pink cotton of her skirts spread across his thighs. He had never seen anything so erotic in his life.

"You slay me, Berries." He kissed all along the column of her throat, loving the way her head lolled back to grant him better access. "I am conquered. Helpless. Undone."

He dug beneath her skirts to cup his hands over her

bottom. God, what an arse she had. Lush and rounded and perfectly sized to fit his large palms. Even through the fabric of her drawers he could feel the perfection of her smooth, warm skin.

"Nick," she sighed, wriggling against his hands. Encouraged, he squeezed, eliciting a little mewl of pleasure.

"Like that, do you?"

"Yes."

He kneaded her soft flesh, catching her moan with his mouth and drawing her closer until the hard length of him was nestled snugly against her sex. She gave a small gasp of surprise, but didn't pull away.

"This is what you do to me, Berries. You drive me wild." His fingers squeezed her buttocks again, and she repeated that delightfully lusty sigh. He kissed down her neck once more, aiming for that tantalizing hint of bosom. "You just tell me when to stop, my sweet. I'll go as far as you like."

Her hands slid up underneath his coat, tugging at the buttons of his waistcoat. "No, don't stop. Please, Nick."

Lovelier words had never been spoken. He would strip her bare, kiss every inch of her skin, shower her with all the pleasure he could give. He wanted to hear her moans and her screams, watch her body contort in ecstasy, thrust deep within her while she begged for more. He would go every bit as far as she would let him.

She had referenced that scandal in her past, so it was possible she had some experience of this nature. It was a question he knew he ought to ask before taking things any further. He could tell that whatever experience she did have was limited, and he wasn't the sort to debauch an innocent.

Except that apparently right now he was. Because he didn't give a damn whether she'd had zero lovers or five thousand. He wanted her, and she wanted him, and that was the only thing that mattered in the world.

He kissed her skin, breathed her in, feasted on her with all his senses.

"God, Berries, you are so damn perfect."

His waistcoat fell open, and she started in on his shirt buttons. "Why don't you ever call me by my real name?"

Nick's entire body went rigid. Berries sat back, eying him with suspicion.

"You never say it. I can't remember you ever saying it. Why not? Do you have a problem with my name?"

"I... I..." He couldn't make the words come out. Half his brain was still stuck on the things he wanted to do to her, the other half on the things she was now sure to do to him.

"Do you even *know* my name?"

The condemned man. Snatched from the brink of heaven and thrown into the depths of hell. He took a deep breath.

"No."

XVIII

By Any Other Name

"*I*'M SO SORRY."

Ida's whole body shook. A choked noise escaped from beneath the hand she'd clapped over her mouth.

"So terribly sorry," Nick continued. "I'm bad with names. Worse than bad. Appallingly awful. It's no excuse, I know. It's my own personal failing." His eyes were fixed on something behind her, sorrow shimmering in their amber depths. "I have wished over and over that I could remember. I'm certain it must be a beautiful name."

Her hand couldn't muffle her snort. His gaze swung back to her, a furrow appearing between his eyebrows.

"Are you…" He blinked several times. "Are you *laughing*?"

The question broke her. The laughter burst out, long and loud, unrestrained and uncontrollable. She fell against his chest, tears of mirth streaming down her cheeks, tremors of hilarity racking her body.

"Oh, goodness." She swiped at her eyes. "Nick, why…"

Another explosion of laughter took her before she could get the question out.

"Why am I so cork-brained?" he offered.

"Yes!"

For several more seconds Ida clung to his shirt, still overcome. Gradually, the shaking stopped, and her breathing returned to normal. She kept her face pressed against his shoulder, afraid that if she looked at him she would lose her composure all over again.

"You truly are cork-brained," she said. "Why didn't you just ask?"

"By the time I realized we wouldn't be quickly parting ways, it was far too late to ask."

She straightened and finally looked him in the eye, frowning. "It's never too late."

"I had hoped someone else would reveal your name, but it never happened in my presence. And you had become Mrs. Masterson or Miss Masterson or anyone other than yourself."

"You should have just asked."

"I felt like a fool."

She giggled again, only just managing to keep it under control. "And now?"

"Now I *know* I'm a fool."

"Well, at least you learned something from all this!"

Nick's laughter began as a tiny sniff, then slowly grew into a deep, rumbling chortle, rising up from his belly to echo throughout the small compartment.

"I certainly did. It's probably for the best that I don't know your name, as I am clearly unworthy to utter it."

"Now you're just being silly."

"A gentleman is never silly."

"Ah, so you're a gentleman, are you? I will add that to the list. Nick Masterson is a gentleman, an inept spy, a potions specialist who doesn't drink them, *not* a gambler or a criminal, and a house decorator."

"Residential designer."

"He is terrible with names but good with kisses."

The big, strong hands that had withdrawn before now grasped her waist. "And what does a young woman of your social class know about a man being good with kisses?"

"I was once a highly-sought heiress. Many men kissed me in the hopes of wedding my fortune."

"And then one of them ruined you."

The edge in his voice made her heart swell. He was angry on her behalf. The first to ever be so. Everyone else had blamed her, though it had been Carsley who had caused the scandal. She never spoke of the incident because all it did was infuriate her. Now, though, she wanted to tell Nick. She wanted to have someone truly listen to her side and believe her.

"Yes."

"Should I know what happened? If I knew your name, would I have heard of your scandal?"

"Only if you move in the same circles as my parents, which is unlikely, I imagine."

"Tell me, then, who are your parents?" He released her waist and grasped both her hands, lifting them to kiss her knuckles. "Berries, my sweet, darling Berries, tell me your real name. Tell me and I will swear to remember."

"Ida Quimby."

"Ida. Ida, Ida, Ida." He kissed her hand each time he said her name. "Ida Quimby. I will repeat your name, Miss Ida Quimby, until even my cork brain can recall it. Lovely Ida. Beautiful Ida. Brave Ida who fights villains with her parasol and saves my fool life. Bold Ida who isn't afraid to sit on my lap and laugh at me. Wonderful Ida who smells like berries and sunshine."

She leaned toward him until their lips brushed. "Sweet Nick who says silly, but flattering things."

"True things." He kissed her mouth, her cheek, and the tip of her nose. "I say only the truth, my Ida. Now, if you will permit me, I will begin to atone for my sins and give you everything you deserve."

He released her hands and began to burrow under her skirts once more. A shiver ran the length of her spine.

"Yes, please."

She couldn't claim to know precisely what he intended, only that she wasn't afraid of it. He would never hurt her, never do anything to her that she didn't desire. And she desired him. Even the slightest touch and her whole body came alive, tightening, heating, yearning for more. Each time his hands and his lips moved closer to forbidden territory she arched into him, hungry, desperate.

His hands found her buttocks again, squeezing in that way that felt so good, that made the place between her legs grow wet. One hand slid along her thigh, sweeping up and over, finding its way to that very spot.

She gasped when his finger stroked through her folds, but the sound soon morphed into a groan of pleasure as his touch sent waves of longing through her. He teased the sensitive little nub—the clitoris, her brother's anatomy textbook had called it—and she pressed against his hand, lost to the mad bliss of it.

"Nick. Oh, Nick. Yes, more," she begged.

"Ida, Ida, Ida," he murmured, his tongue tickling her neck and her shoulder where her dress was slipping down. When had he unbuttoned it?

"Oh, please." She clutched at his shirt, anchoring herself to him when the yearning building inside her threatened to split her apart. The last button popped off, and the shirt tore open, exposing the curls of dark hair over his pale skin.

"Nick," she gasped. Her head fell against his now half-bare chest, her cheek pressed to his warm flesh. "I can't… I need…" She didn't even know what she needed, only that it was there, so close, and somehow just beyond her grasp.

The hand between her thighs continued stroking, tormenting, pleasuring, while his opposite arm curled around her, cradling her, sheltering her.

"Come for me, Berries."

The world cracked. Her body spasmed in absolute rapture, rocketing up from the earth and then floating slowly, ever so slowly back down to earth, where Nick held her in his arms and pressed gentle kisses to her mouth.

"Sweet, sweet Ida," he murmured. "Do you forgive me?"

"Yes," she sighed. "For everything. Anything."

He chuckled. "Perhaps I will ask again when you have come down from the euphoria."

Ida closed her eyes and snuggled close to him, smelling his comforting scent, nuzzling her cheek against his short whiskers. "I will still say yes. Always yes."

XIX

The Scandalous Miss Quimby

Nick frowned down at his pocket watch, reading the numbers for the third time. His mind couldn't process the calculations that usually came so easily. What day was it again? This morning felt like a lifetime ago.

Nine days, seventeen hours, three minutes.

He wouldn't count the potions Berries had used to heal him. He hadn't drunk them, and he hadn't experienced any sort of mental alterations or cravings as a result. By the time he'd awakened, it had been as if nothing had ever happened.

The second hand ticked steadily along. Was he deluding himself? Would starting over make more sense?

Nick closed the watch and jammed it into his pocket. Did it even matter? He was successfully avoiding potions. Only the single relapse thus far. Berries—Ida—had neither shunned him nor pitied him, merely accepted. He had a vision for his future. One that went beyond potion parties and late-night card games.

One that included the blond-haired beauty that lay sprawled across the narrow train bed, sleeping off the effects of her eventful morning.

He had pulled the armchair close enough that he could touch her, but had so far resisted the impulse to do so. She deserved her rest, and he needed the time to think things over. For now, it was enough to look upon her and admire the aftermath of their passionate embrace.

A few stray curls had come loose from their pins, framing her face and spilling across the pillow. Her bodice was askew, exposing the trim along the top of her corset. It was, as he had suspected, delightfully pink. He'd never had much use for the color pink, but now it would forever remind him of her.

My lovely Ida. Miss Ida Qui… Quimby.

He needed to practice her surname. It wouldn't do to wake up tomorrow having forgotten it all over again. Even if it was the least important part of her name. Soon enough she would be Ida Masterson, Countess of Sharpe.

Nick had no idea when or how he'd gone and fallen in love with her, but here he was, wanting to throw himself at her feet and beg to do her bidding. He would get her safely to India, get that serum from her brother, even if he had to pummel the man to do it, and then scurry back to London for the hastiest wedding he could arrange. He'd already penned a note to his mother, and he'd drop it at the telegraph office the moment they reached Suez.

This all assumed, of course, that Ida would accept his proposal. She might think him completely mad. What sort of woman married a man she'd met on a train and known for less than two weeks?

His sort, hopefully.

He needed her to accept him. He craved her with every fiber of his being. He would do all he could to make himself worthy of her. The steamer to Bombay took thirteen days. He would spend each one wooing her. And protecting her from stalkers and knife-wielding thugs.

She stirred beside him, stretching her limbs and rubbing her eyes. Nick took in every twist of her body, every sleepy noise. His cock began to stiffen again, as he imagined how he might ravish her, and fully this time. He scooted the chair away from the bed. He wouldn't rush her. Passionate as she was, he doubted the wait would be too terrible.

Ida yawned. "How long did I sleep?"

"Thirty-seven minutes."

She sat up, tugging her dress into place. "That is very exact."

"I check the time often."

"Yes, I have observed that nervous habit of yours." Long delicate fingers closed the buttons of her bodice, hiding that hint of her undergarments. Another day he'd strip all those layers away. "Did you forget my name again while I was sleeping?"

"Miss Ivy Quigley, correct?" His attempt at a straight face failed catastrophically, and they both burst out laughing. "Ida. Ida Quimby. I remember."

"Good. So now you know who I am."

"No more than I did before. I merely have a second name by which to call you."

"You haven't heard of my father?"

Nick's brows knitted together. "Should I have?"

"Sir Mortimer Quimby."

"That does sound familiar."

"He was knighted for his work designing and building a fleet of ships for the Imperial Potions Company."

Memories fell into place. The party. Sir Mortimer's library. "Sir Boatbuilder of the Glowing Wallpaper is your father?"

Her cheeks colored. "Yes, he is. I hate that wallpaper."

Nick raked a hand through his hair. "Bloody hell."

"So you do know my family, then." Her eyes fell to the floor. "You know my scandal."

He grabbed her hand, holding it in both of his. "No, I don't. Nor do I care. I'm only stunned because I was in your house."

"What?"

"I was at his party, two nights before we met. I was there, in your house, and I had no idea. No idea that you were there. No idea that you even existed."

No idea that the love of my life hovered so very near.

"I stay in my room during the parties. I never liked them much in the first place, and since the scandal my parents would prefer that people forget I exist."

"Tell me about it."

She withdrew her hand and slid back on the bed, putting more distance between them. "I get angry thinking about it. Don't take it personally."

"I won't."

"I told you I had many suitors and I liked to kiss them. People knew that, but I didn't think it mattered. Minorly scandalous. Nothing worth putting in the papers. But I apparently had a 'reputation.'

"My father was pushing for a betrothal to Lord Carsley, part of a business arrangement where Carsley's father would invest in a new shipbuilding venture."

Nick's posture stiffened. *Ida* was the woman his friend Carsley had almost married? Nick hadn't thought much about it at the time. Carsley had shrugged off being jilted, saying she wasn't worth fussing over. Was he out of his mind? Losing her was the most devastating thing Nick could imagine. He fought for composure, needing to hear what had happened.

"I can't get behind a man selling his daughter in a business deal," he said, surprising himself with the evenness of his tone, "but at least Carsley is a decent sort."

"No, he's not."

Nick's jaw dropped open. "He's one of my best friends."

Ida shrank back against the wall, her shoulders drooping. "Never mind."

He started to reach for her, but stopped with his hand in

mid-air, letting it drop before speaking. "No, please go on. Tell me why you dislike him."

"You won't believe me. No one does." Her words were jagged. Sorrow, laced with venom. His sweet, wounded Berries. He wanted to wrap her up in his arms and hold her forever.

"Tell me. Please."

She looked back up and breathed deeply. "I liked Carsley. He was charming. Funny. Amiable. Handsome and a good dancer."

"I can't speak for his dancing skills, but I have known him to be all those other things."

"I thought maybe this arranged marriage could work, and I spent a lot of time with him, hoping to get to know him better. I kissed him a number of times. He also would pinch my bottom, usually without warning." Her cheeks flamed. "I didn't stop him because I liked it.

"Things were going well, both with the business deal and between us, and at one of my father's parties we snuck off for some kisses. He wanted it to go further. I didn't. I knew it would be more than just a few whispers if we were caught doing anything like that, and I didn't feel that I was ready, if that makes any sense."

"It does. We are each ready in our own time."

"I told him that, and he just laughed. He didn't grab me or touch me, but he blocked the door, and he kept trying to talk me into it. I said 'no' I don't know how many times. He wouldn't listen, telling me it was going to happen, whatever I said, trying to bully me into it. He moved closer and closer as he talked. I didn't think I could get past him out the door, and I knew if he became physical he was much stronger than I was. So I screamed."

"Jesus."

She didn't even call Nick out for his blasphemy, she was so wrapped up in her emotional tale.

"People came running. I told them what had happened.

He called me hysterical. It only got worse from there. When someone said that none of it mattered because we were expected to marry, I refused him. Right there in public and very loudly. Suddenly, I was a jilter. A temptress who had led him on. It was *my own fault*, they said, that I was compromised.

"My parents tried to smooth things over, wishing to salvage the business deal, but I would not speak anything but the truth, and nothing could have compelled me to reconcile with Carsley. The deal collapsed. My father was livid. Several men offered to wed me despite my 'soiled state' to get at my fortune. I also refused them, much to my family's dismay. I was still going out at the time, thinking surely someone would take my side and see that I wasn't the wrongdoer. Instead, I was snubbed and mocked while Carsley was as popular as ever. Men laughed with him. Women flirted with him. *Everyone* believed him.

"One day I had had enough. I walked up to him at the last party I ever attended, dumped my champagne over his head, and announced to the world that I would rather be a ruined woman than a..." She cleared her throat. "Than a 'lecherous, bum-pinching, lying sack of shit.'"

Ida let out a long, slow breath and folded her hands in her lap. "So, there you have it. The full and true story of my scandal."

Nick's mind reeled. He couldn't wrap his head around the image of Carsley hurting anyone. They had been friends since age ten. He'd had Nick's back during countless wild parties. They'd often spent time together admiring the young ladies in attendance. Now each of those memories carried a sick taint. How many of those women had been victims of unwanted advances?

The pain of betrayal cut Nick as deeply as the knife in his gut, but this wound had no potions to heal it. How could someone he'd loved like a brother be so barbaric?

"Nick?"

The uncertainty in her voice jolted him. He looked her straight in the eye and held out his hand, leaving it up to her whether to take it.

"I believe you. I hope that I would believe anyone. We men hold all the power, and it is only too easy to abuse it." Her fingers closed around his. "It kills me that I didn't know. That I sat and played cards with him. Laughed with him. Knowing how much this hurts me, I can't even comprehend how much more it must have hurt you."

Her thumb traced gentle strokes across the back of his hand. "Thank you."

"How did you not murder me for that kidnapping stunt?"

"Oh, I considered it."

"You should have done it. You should have left me to die on the streets of Alexandria like the worthless refuse I am."

"Don't be ridiculous. You were foolish and arrogant, but not cruel. Your motivation saved you. I never had any doubt that you believed you were coming to my rescue."

"I was a jackass."

A slight smile touched her lips. "I don't disagree."

"I will spend the rest of my life begging your forgiveness."

"Didn't I already say I forgave you?"

"You were distracted."

She edged closer. "I wouldn't mind being distracted again."

Nick sprang from his seat, lifting her up from the bed into a fierce embrace. His lips hovered a breath away from hers when a sharp crack rent the air outside their compartment.

He whirled toward the door, shielding her body with his own. A heavy silence fell, the rhythmic clack of the train the only sound cutting through the stillness. Nick stepped to the door and slid it open. The scent of gunpowder filled the narrow hall.

"Here." Berries gestured at a hole in the wall of the corridor, where a bullet had lodged in the wooden paneling.

"And there's a note."

Nick scooped up the scrap of paper from the floor. The pasted-on bits of newsprint read, *Last Warning.*

He ushered Ida back into the room and closed the door behind them, dragging the armchair in front of the entrance for added security.

"I should have hired a bodyguard," he muttered.

She frowned at him. "How does one go about hiring such a person?"

"I haven't the foggiest. My uncle would know, but anyone he sent would be weeks behind us." Nick shook his head ruefully. "I will escort you home if you desire. Or continue on with you. Your choice. This is your expedition."

"What of your own mission?"

"I quit. It's not worth my life."

Ida thought a moment before replying. "I want to keep going."

It took every ounce of his self-control not to say the words that pounded through his brain.

No. Don't. Go home. Be safe.

He looked away from her, clenching his fists to still his trembling hands. "So be it."

XX

Ill Temper

IDA DUNKED THE CLOTH INTO the cool water, wrung it out, and then laid it across the back of Nick's neck. He didn't flinch, but she heard the sharp hiss of his breath—a far more pleasant sound than his earlier groans of misery.

"Thank you," he mumbled.

"You are most welcome. How are you feeling? Any improvement?"

A grunt was his only reply.

"Our luncheon should arrive shortly. I requested some dry toast, if you think you could stomach that."

As if the mere thought of food were enough to make him ill, Nick dove for the side of the bed, retching into the chamber pot for what seemed the thousandth time since the ship had left port that morning.

"Or not."

She retrieved the damp cloth, and when he rolled onto his back she mopped the sweat from his brow.

"Are you certain you won't take a potion? I could feed you only a spoonful or two and keep the rest away."

"No. If I taste the serum the cravings will become overwhelming, and I'm not in the best state to handle them."

"You've had no food all day, and yet you continue to be sick. I'm worried you will soon have no insides left at all."

She swiped the cloth along his cheek and down his neck. She had long since deprived him of his necktie and undone the top button of his shirt. Not that she was certain it had made any difference. Sometimes, like now, his skin was warm and flushed, while at other times he seemed cold. All she could do was attempt to keep him comfortable.

Nick reached up to stroke a finger down her cheek.

"You are good to me, Berries."

"I only wish there was more I could do. Shall I read to you? Or would you like to try to sleep? I can even fetch you that little rabbit if it will be a comfort."

"Pardon?"

"The little toy rabbit from your trunk. I found it when I went looking for something to read. It must be very special to you if you carry it around when you travel."

Nick swore and rolled onto his stomach.

"You needn't be embarrassed on my account. Sentimental items are part of our basic human nature, I believe."

He turned back over slowly, grimacing and putting a hand to his belly. "I was given that toy when my sister, Anna, was born. It reminds me of her."

"Ah. You two are close?"

"Very. But she was recently married and I haven't seen her in months."

"You must miss her."

"I do. Anna the rabbit has never been as good as Anna the person."

"You gave her your sister's name? That's sweet."

"Yes, except that Anna the rabbit is a boy rabbit. Which caused some childhood disagreements, as did my tendency to adorn him with sparkly ribbons."

"Well, I'm of the firm opinion that we all ought to be our true selves rather than what we are told to be. If he wishes to wear pretty things and have a girl's name, who am I to judge?"

Nick smiled for the first time that day. "You are a treasure, Miss Ida Quimby."

A knock at the door saved her from stammering a bashful thanks.

"That would be our lunch. Well, *my* lunch. Perhaps you might have a bit of tea at least? What if I put a few drops of potion into it? Would that mask the serum enough for you to safely drink it?"

He shook his head. "I would notice, even if you did it in secret."

"I promise to do no such thing. Excuse me, I must go to the door."

Ida pushed herself up off the bed and slipped the steak knife—which she now thought of as hers—from her travel satchel. Holding it behind her back, she cracked open the door. She would take no chances. She and Nick would stay together at all times, behind locked doors whenever possible, and she would remain alert for any possibility of an attack.

"Ida?"

She waved off his question and opened the door fully to allow the man with her lunch tray to enter, keeping hold of her knife in case he was an enemy in disguise. He placed the tray on the small table.

"Here you are, Mrs. Masterson. Is there anything else I can do for you?"

"No, that is quite sufficient, thank you."

"Very good."

He bowed and departed. The tension drained from Ida's muscles when the lock fell back into place. She dropped the knife into her bag and lowered herself onto the edge of the bed.

"Ida?" Nick's question now carried a heavy dose of suspicion. "Why are you wielding a knife?"

"Someone has to protect you in the event of an attack. You are in no state to do so yourself."

"I understand your concern, but why do you even *have* a knife? Did you steal it from a kitchen somewhere?"

"Er…" Ida couldn't meet his eyes. She would have to confess, and then he would be both angry and worried for her. Neither of which he needed right now.

He levered himself up on one elbow. "I would have bought you a knife if you had asked. Or better yet, taught you to use my defensive potions. I have many of them, and they can keep you safe with no need for weapons."

"I didn't steal it. I, well, found it. I'm sorry. I should have told you, but I worried you would panic and try to send me home."

He sat fully upright, the movement causing him to grimace and clutch his stomach. "Found it where? Berries, what's going on?"

Ida exhaled slowly. "I found it stabbed into my pillow when we boarded the ship to Alexandria."

"What?" He lunged toward her. "Someone was in your room? Someone was in your room *with a weapon* and you didn't tell me?"

"I took precautions. I locked and barricaded the door every night."

"You could have been killed!" His normally low voice had risen nearly a full octave. "For Christ's sake, Ida, what if someone had gotten in? What if something had happened to you?"

"Nothing did happen. Please, lie back down, you are looking very unwell." She scanned the bed around him. "Where did I leave that damp cloth?"

Nick didn't stop ranting. "How could you not tell me? You could have died and I wouldn't have been there to save you."

"Lie down, please, before you make yourself worse." Ida

put her hands on his shoulders to push him back down, but he was too strong to move even an inch.

He grasped both her wrists. "Berries, look at me. What if I had lost you? What would I do without you? I can't… I can't even think, I can't even imagine. God, Berries, what would I do?"

"Hush. Nick, please, you are sounding delirious and you have gone a ghastly shade of white. Please rest. Please. I'm fine. I'm here."

His grip relaxed and he slumped onto the bed, groaning, though she couldn't tell whether from illness or merely ill temper. She found the cloth, rewet it, and bathed his face and neck. His breathing began to slow, and color returned to his cheeks.

"There you are," she murmured. "Everything will be well. Neither of us is harmed."

His arms wrapped around her waist and he pulled her down on top of him.

"I don't understand," he said, laying his head against hers. "Why would anyone wish to hurt you?"

"I wish I knew."

"I swear, Berries, I swear I will protect you with every last breath in my body."

"We will protect one another." She closed her eyes and let herself bask a moment in the warmth and passion of his embrace. "I'm sorry."

"Why didn't you tell me?"

"I should have, but I knew you would react badly. I knew you would become upset the way you are now. And I was still rather furious with you at the time. You'd given me no real indication that you thought kidnapping me was wrong. I feared you would become so concerned for my safety that you would drag me back home."

His fingers twined in her hair. "I knew it was wrong from the start. I was only ever making excuses. I'm so sorry."

He really was going to be apologizing for the rest of his

life. It amused her, but also left her with a feeling of deep satisfaction.

"Would it be so bad?" he asked. "Going home? There are other things you could have done. You could purchase your serum from the usual suppliers."

"It's too expensive in the quantities I need to get my business started. I was relying on Alfred's connections."

"But you are an heiress. Where has your money gone? If your family has disowned you, I will give your father a piece of my mind."

"No, the money has gone nowhere. I haven't touched it. I don't want to touch it. I have planned for this business using only what I already have—a small inheritance from an aunt a number of years ago and what I saved from my allowances. I have budgeted everything so that I needn't ask for any money. Not from my dowry, not from anyone. I plan to find a house of my own someday, buy my own food and clothes. I will be entirely independent. No one's burden but my own."

Nick planted a kiss among the tangled mess that had until recently been her hairdo. "You could never be a burden. You are so strong, so full of purpose and full of life. There is no one I admire more."

She murmured his name, her voice choked with emotion, unable to form other words.

"There are things I must tell you," he said. "Things I should have said long ago. I can't blame you for not telling me all. Not when I have done the same. I've given you so little of myself."

Ida sat up as best she could in his embrace, once again caressing his cheek with her cloth. "Another time. You are ill, and I have caused you great distress just now. Rest, and we will talk later."

His eyes closed and he breathed a long sigh. "Thank you. I am tired."

She wriggled out of his arms until she lay beside him,

one arm draped across his chest. "I will hold you until you are asleep."

"No, don't. You will be here too long."

A few minutes later, when his breathing had settled into a slow, steady rhythm, Ida slipped from the bed and sat down at the small table to take her lunch. She set one of Nick's healing potions beside her plate before picking up her sandwich. She didn't think her food was likely to be poisoned, but she would take no chances.

She would protect herself and Nick from any and all harm. Whatever it took.

XXI

Rank and Title

"ENOUGH," NICK GROWLED.

Berries scowled up at him, the knight piece still clasped in her hand. She surveyed him across the chessboard. The same damned chessboard that had sat atop the same damned table for three bloody days. If he didn't get out of this cabin soon he was going to go stark raving mad.

"You made me lose my train of thought," she said. "Now I have to go through it all over again. If I move him and you move your bishop, then it sets up the possibility for me to take him, but only if I wish to expose another piece. If I don't capture—"

"Stop, I beg you, before I overturn the board."

"I'm trying to make a good game of it. If we go too fast we will have to play again and again."

"We have already played again and again. I'm going mad with boredom, and so are you."

She lifted her chin proudly. "Nonsense."

"Look at those wrinkles in your skirts from where you have been crushing them in your fists. You are restless and agitated. But enough is enough. We are going out."

Ida glanced down at her lap, then quickly back up at him. "Nick, we can't. I thought we agreed that we must remain safe. Only leaving the cabin for food and to use the washroom, never alone. Otherwise in the cabin with the door barricaded."

He rose abruptly, rattling the board and knocking over several pieces. In the voice he usually reserved for the floor of Parliament, he repeated, "We are going out."

She was on her feet a moment later, the game forgotten. "You needn't be so tyrannical."

Nick's jaw clenched. Did she hate his authoritative side? She probably hated it. Dammit so much.

He couldn't help himself. He was accustomed to making decisions and giving orders. It was a necessary part of his life. The part of his life she didn't know about. Damn, damn, damn.

"Would you listen to me otherwise?" he challenged.

"I'm not listening to you now. I'm perfectly fine here. We can read one of your books. Again. Or start up another game of cards. Do you know any magic tricks?"

He pushed the dressing table barricade out of the way and opened the door. Ida darted into the corridor, looking this way and that, her steak knife clutched in her hand, ready to defend him to the death. God, what a woman.

"It does appear safe enough," she said, slipping the knife back into her purse.

"You are going mad, and so am I."

"I know, but..."

"You can't keep me shut away forever, Ida. Nor can I do such to you."

Her sigh was long and heavy. "Oh, very well. But we must stay in public spaces where we can be seen at all times and cannot be attacked, and you must tell me all about your defensive potions. Perhaps we can even look for clues. Do you know how to do that?"

"No. My sister is the investigator in the family. With as little as we know, I don't even know where to start." He locked the door and double-checked it before extending his hand. "Come. Let's walk about the deck. I fear my legs will stop working entirely if I don't stretch them out. I'll tell you about those potions."

Her fingers twined with his, the touch igniting a blaze of desire deep within him. Three days they'd been together in that cabin. Three nights lying side-by-side on the small bed. And yet this was their most intimate contact since she'd nursed him through his seasickness. He fought off the temptation to turn right around and usher her back into the bedroom.

They walked hand-in-hand up to the deck, eyes too long indoors squinting in the bright sunshine. The gentle breeze ruffled Nick's never-tidy hair and toyed with a little curl that had escaped Ida's chignon. He considered tucking it behind her ear. Running his thumb across her cheek. Tugging her close for a long, lingering kiss. Sating the desire that had been driving him mad for days.

Not in public. The weather was too fine. Many men, and a handful of women besides, strolled the deck, basking in the warmth of the sunshine. He couldn't do anything here that might be construed as inappropriate. Not after what Berries had already suffered at the hands of "good society." Instead he tried to keep watch for Thin-Face and the Fauxmericans.

"Tell me about the potions," Ida suggested.

Potions. Yes. Anything to keep his mind off of her. Anything not to dwell on the glimpses of bare leg he'd seen as she slid in and out of the bed. Or the way her nightgown clung to the perfect curves of her breasts.

He kept his eyes fixed firmly ahead, but her delicate scent of rose and bergamot wafted through the air, teasing and tempting. A perfect blend of masculine and feminine, it slithered through his defenses, conjuring up fantasies of other, more corporeal joinings.

"You've seen the sleeping potion." His voice sounded unnaturally low. He released her hand before she could notice his palm had begun to sweat. "I cleaned and refilled the syringe. We must be sparing with it, however, as that is all I have left of it."

"I would hope it would be a last resort. I would prefer you never get close enough to an attacker to use it. It didn't work out well for you in Alexandria."

"I lived."

Thanks to her. If he'd been alone, would he have had sense enough to treat the wound? Or could he have brought himself to drink one of the other healing potions? He honestly didn't know.

Nick reached inside his coat, finding the potion he desired by feel alone. "I imagine this looks familiar to you."

Ida accepted the small bottle, examining the pump mechanism. "A common enough style of perfume bottle. But I assume this is not a fragrance."

"No. It's meant to stun. Any enemy who inhales the mist will be rendered momentarily confused and dizzy. A larger dose and he will collapse. It's easy to use, but you must be certain of the wind conditions so you don't inhale any yourself. Best used indoors where the air is still."

She returned the potion and he swapped it for the next.

"Slick potion. Pour out behind you if you are being chased. Nine times out of ten a person stepping in it will fall. I have two, and they are both in these green vials."

"Green vials. Understood."

"Finally, I have a flash potion. Only one, in this tear-drop shaped bottle. Expose it to air, and it will produce a flash of light bright enough to temporarily blind a man. Dash it on the ground and don't look."

She nodded.

"Would you like to carry any with you?"

"One slick potion, in case we must run. I will leave the rest to you, since we will be remaining together at all times."

She gave him a stern look, warning him that any misbehavior

would have consequences. It was a look of authority, one that few would dare use on a man of his rank.

Not that she knew who he really was. He'd tried to tell her over the last few days, as he regaled her with tales of his childhood, but each time the words clogged in his throat. He couldn't bear to change her image of him. Now he was Mr. Masterson, residential designer and sometime investigative agent. A gentleman, but one who plied a trade. They were equals.

The moment he became Lord Sharpe, the power balance would shift. He could only imagine what her social-climbing parents must have taught her about interacting with titled ladies and gentlemen. Deference, mildness, excessive courtesy. Suppression of her natural exuberance. He couldn't imagine her being anything but disdainful of such advice. After her ill-treatment by Carsley and others of his social circle, she would have all the more reason to resent the aristocracy.

She already disliked his tendency to give orders with every expectation of immediate obedience. How furious would she be to find that it came from a decade of commanding an earldom? And he could hardly undo his situation in life.

"There is something I must tell you. About myself."

Ida's nose crinkled as she frowned. "You make it sound so dire. Haven't you been telling me about yourself for days? All those stories about you and Anna. How you left university to become the protector of your family when your father died. Sweet things and admirable things. You are a good man, Nicholas Masterson. A gentleman not merely in the traditional sense, but by your actions and your integrity."

But he *was* a gentleman in the traditional sense. A landowner with no need to work for a living. A man whose primary business was to pay his estate manager and the bankers who organized the investments that slowly, but steadily, increased his family fortune. A man who was supposed to feel superior to the scandalous daughter of a mere knighted tradesman.

Dammit, he didn't want to tell her. He didn't want to outrank her.

"You're too good for me, Ida Quimby."

"Excuse me, did you say 'Quimby'?" interrupted an unfamiliar voice. Both Nick and Ida spun to look at the speaker, a pristinely-dressed young man with a curled moustache and slicked-back hair.

"Er, yes. I am Miss Quimby."

"Are you a relation to Sir Mortimer Quimby?"

"He is my father, in fact."

A wide smile split the man's face. "How wonderful! I didn't know he had a daughter. Of course, I have known him less than a year, and not as well as I would like. But he is a capital fellow! Throws wonderful parties. So generous to his guests. But forgive me, I haven't introduced myself. Mr. John Featherstone, at your service. Such a pleasure to make your acquaintance, Miss Quimby."

"Oh, thank you." She glanced at Nick. "Allow me to…"

"You must come to the ball I am hosting, Miss Quimby," the interrupter babbled. "Nothing so grand as your father's parties of course, just a small affair I'm putting on, but the ballroom here on the ship is adequate and we will have drinks and music and dancing. You must save me a dance, Miss Quimby. Now, tell, me, what brings you so far from home?"

He reached to take her arm, but Ida deftly dodged his touch.

"I'm on my way to visit my brother, who works in Bombay."

"Ah, wonderful, wonderful. Family is so important, don't you think? I do hope your travels have been pleasant."

"As a matter of fact, they have been. I was able to spend some time in Paris, and after a rather unexpected detour…" She tossed Nick a significant look. "I had a few days of sightseeing in Italy."

She would never stop reminding him. The thought almost made him smile. He would happily suffer a lifetime of reminders if it meant a lifetime with her.

"Excellent! That is such a fetching ensemble you are wearing, Miss Quimby. The pink brings out the color in your cheeks."

Nick scowled, not that Interrupter noticed, or even looked in his direction. He was too busy goggling at Berries, his eyes sweeping up and down her figure.

"And that scent you are wearing is so delightful."

Now the scoundrel was smelling her? Nick's jaw tightened. Why hadn't he had the sense to compliment her on the new perfume before anyone else did?

Ida's blue eyes glimmered with happiness. "Thank you. I made it myself. It's a new fragrance that I'm testing for the first time."

"It is very much a success."

The man leaned toward her, breathing deeply, and Nick was struck with an unusually violent urge to smash the cad's pretty nose.

"Do tell me you will attend my little ball," the jackass continued. "It is to be held the last night of our journey, so I have called it the Twelfth Night ball and it will have a Shakespearean theme, because who doesn't like the Bard?"

"A ball does sound nice. It has been too long since I danced."

The wistfulness of her tone cut straight to Nick's heart. She hadn't been to a party in two years, and he knew she loved to dance. He'd seen her twirling down the streets often enough, moving to music that existed only in her head. Damn it all, she was going to this ball and he was going to make certain she had the time of her life.

"We would be happy to accept your invitation," he said, loud enough that Interrupter could no longer ignore him.

The man turned slowly. His eyes scanned Nick from head

to toe, taking in the scuffed boots, faded coat, and two days' worth of stubble.

"My invitation was extended only to the lady, sir." He put a heavy sneer on the last word, looking down his nose even though he fell several inches short of Nick's height.

"My lord," Nick corrected.

"I beg your pardon?"

"I believe you meant to say, 'My invitation was extended only to the lady, my lord, but I would be most honored if you would grace us with your presence as well.'"

Interrupter puffed up his scrawny chest. "Just who do you think you are?"

Nick strode closer until he loomed over the smaller man. Putting the full weight of his noble lineage into his voice, he replied, "Nicholas Masterson, Earl of Sharpe."

XXII

That Wicked Waltz

IDA SHOVED HER VERY LAST HAIRPIN into her coiffure, catching the last stray wisp she could see in the looking glass. She didn't know whether it would hold up through a whole night of dancing, but it was the best she could do. She was lucky she'd brought the pink and black dress with the separate evening bodice. Her original itinerary had certainly not included any balls. Then again, nothing about this journey had gone as expected.

A knock sounded at the door.

"Come in."

She watched the door in the mirror, her hand poised to grab her knife, just in case.

"You didn't lock the door," Nick growled.

"You went out on your own," she retorted. "Why should I abide by the terms of our agreement when you don't? Oh, but I forget, you always have to have things your own way."

"Whereas you are so biddable and demure." He heaved a sigh. "Forgive me, that was inconsiderate. I don't wish you to be other than you are."

Would it ever end, this snipping at one another? Ida was tired of the awkwardness, tired of feeling anxious and short-tempered. Every day it seemed they had less to say to one another. They walked the deck in silence, spoke of nothing but the food at every meal, and spent too much time sitting in their cabin, staring at books they'd already read and avoiding even the slightest touch.

She studied her reflection, pretending to adjust her hairdo. Anything to keep from turning around and looking at him. Tomorrow it would all be over. She would be in India, ready to confront her brother, and Nick—Lord Sharpe, she reminded herself for the millionth time—would do whatever it was he needed to do for his own mission. Or he'd turn around and go home, if he'd been serious about quitting.

This wasn't how it was supposed to end. She longed for the days when they hadn't fully known each other. When she'd still been Berries to him and he'd been no more than a mister. When she'd entertained secret fantasies of adorable, amber-eyed children and a modest townhouse in a quiet neighborhood where he would design her a pretty little workshop for her perfume business.

At least she understood now why he hadn't touched her since that wild, wanton day when he'd learned her name. Earls didn't marry ruined daughters of tradesmen. And Nick was too good a person to do anything he thought would constitute taking advantage of her. He probably regretted what they'd already done in the throes of passion.

She couldn't even be angry with him for hiding the truth. Not when she'd kept important secrets of her own. And what had the truth brought them except frustration and sorrow?

Nick cleared his throat. "Are you ready to go, or do you need a moment?"

Ida slid from the chair, smoothing out her skirts as she rose, and turning to face him. "I'm r-ready."

Or she had been, a moment ago. The moment before she'd

seen him. Now, though, she was frozen, her feet glued to the floor where she stood, unable to do anything but stare. She'd known he had gone out for a shave and a haircut, and that he intended to change into evening attire. What she'd never considered was that the transformation would be so drastic.

How had she ever thought him an unimportant sort of man? Every inch of him radiated money and power. Gone were the battered coat and the sturdy boots. His new ensemble was nothing short of perfect, from the gleam of his dancing shoes to the pristine white gloves and the intricately knotted necktie. His tailcoat fit him so exactly that she wondered how he'd even gotten into it.

She willed herself to say something, in the hopes that freeing her tongue would unstick the rest of her.

"You look ravishing," she blurted.

No. No. That was absolutely the wrong thing to say. Never mind that she wanted to kiss him hard enough to rumple his perfection. To drag him out into public and say to the world, *See this magnificent man? He's* mine.

If only.

"Ravishing." The deep tremor of his voice caused a quiver low in her belly. His eyes had turned to liquid gold, and her body began to move again, melted by the heat of his gaze. "Twirl for me, ravishing Ida."

He motioned for her to spin, and she did, showing off the evening bodice, with its flattering neckline and daringly low back. She couldn't wear a corset with it, but even beneath his smoldering stare she didn't feel unclothed. Instead she felt brazen and powerful. A match for the blue-blooded man in front of her.

"I claim your first waltz," he said.

"Not the first dance?"

"Let some other fool sashay about in little squares of four, barely touching you. I want to hold you. We will waltz."

Here was her chance, it seemed, to claim him in front of everyone. "I will put your name on my dance card."

"Good. Shall we go?"

"Please."

How she managed to walk all the way to the ballroom without kissing him, she didn't know. For twelve days she'd suffered the pangs of pent-up desire. She'd turned her back while he dressed and slept perched on the edge of the bed, trying to focus on keeping him safe instead of on the way his hands and lips had felt upon her skin.

Tonight, though. Tonight in her elegant clothing, attending her first party in years, the desire had broken loose. Perhaps for this one night she could live the fairy tale.

The moment they stepped into the ballroom, men swarmed her. Ladies were in short supply on the ship. Over the past week, Featherstone had introduced Ida to a number of women traveling with their husbands to new situations in India. They would make fine dancing partners, certainly, but the rare unmarried women were the true draw for the men in attendance tonight. Ida spied two young women, barely out of the schoolroom, here with their fathers. They were joined by half-a-dozen unaccompanied women who had struck out from home in search of husbands. Likely seen as wallflowers or spinsters in London, here they would be the center of attention. And once in India, they would have their pick of British officers.

Ida was younger than all the husband hunters and, she now realized, wearing a dress that was far more expensive and fashionable than any other. After Nick, she was the highest ranking and wealthiest person here. Men flocked to her.

She hurriedly scribbled Nick's name onto her dance card, then held it behind her back to prevent anyone from grabbing at it. Featherstone pushed his way to her side, grabbing her free hand and kissing it.

"Miss Quimby. You look ravishing."

She disliked that word on his lips. Only one man here could interest her in ravishment, but Nick had been surrounded by women in the same way that she had fallen prey to the men. Ida wondered if either of them would manage an escape.

"You must permit me to claim that dance," Featherstone murmured, still clinging to her hand.

"Er, yes." Ida twisted her hand until he had no choice but to let go. "Perhaps the quadrille. I shall have to check my dance card. Ah, but first I'm in need of some refreshment. Excuse me." She spun away, squeezing through the throng of admirers who could only see décolletage and money.

The only drink available was a *goût français* champagne, which she knew would taste unpleasantly sweet. Hardly the fortifying libation she had hoped for, but she took a glass regardless. Perhaps if she downed it quickly it would relax her. As she lifted the flute to her lips, a white-gloved hand appeared in front of her, holding a metal flask.

"Whisky?"

"Yes, please." She abandoned the champagne and instead took a long pull from the flask. The smooth, oaky liquor carried precisely the right amount of burn, warming her insides. "This is excellent."

Nick grinned. "Anna married a whisky manufacturer."

"Really? I would have expected a duke or somesuch."

"Eligible dukes are in short supply."

Ida took a second swig of the whisky before handing it back. "Honestly, I paid almost zero attention to my mother's lectures on the peerage and haven't any idea which lords I've met are barons or marquesses or what have you."

"I'm not in the least surprised. Let me see that dance card of yours. Your admirers are headed this way, and I won't allow them to monopolize all your time."

"I put your name down already. First waltz."

The tiny, attached pencil looked ridiculous in Nick's large

hand, but he managed to scrawl something on the card before returning it.

"That will do, I suppose."

Ida gaped at the card, then up at him. "Three dances?" All waltzes. The first, the last, and one in the middle. "With so few ladies to go around?"

"I prefer there be no doubts as to my intentions."

She picked a random spot on the floor to stare at, afraid to meet his eyes. Because if his expression carried even half the intensity of his voice, she might forever become That Woman Who Kissed the Earl of Sharpe in Full View of Everyone.

"And what intentions would those be, my lord?" Perhaps the cool politeness would help slow her hammering heart. He couldn't really mean to court her. She must be misunderstanding.

"Firstly, I intend for you never to address me with such formality ever again."

She lifted her head and her heart skipped a beat. The rest of the world had dimmed and she could see only her Nick with the amber eyes that seemed to penetrate into her very soul. Improbably handsome, impossibly sweet, and dangerously, kissably close.

"Miss Quimby!"

Ida jumped.

"The dancing is about to begin, and I must claim that dance while I still have the opportunity," Featherstone gabbed. "Would you do me the honor?"

"Er, yes. Of course."

Nick gave her a nod. "I will see you for that waltz."

Ida didn't hear a single word of what Featherstone said during their dance. She nodded and smiled and moved about in a daze until Nick came to sweep her into his arms.

"I'm so sorry, Ida," he murmured, the low purr of his voice a caress against her skin.

"Sorry?"

Was he not making sense, or could her brain simply not

process words while her body burned? He had overwhelmed every one of her senses. He smelled of lemon-scented shaving soap and a hint of whisky. Warmth radiated from his body, and his strong arm drew her inappropriately close. The supple leather of his evening gloves skimmed across her bare back, searing her skin.

"I have made a hash of everything. I wanted only to give you space, to leave you free to choose your own path, and yet all I have done is push you away. I should have been up front with you from the beginning. You have every right to be angry..."

"About your title? I'm not. I was startled, at first, but it doesn't matter. It doesn't change who you are. You are beautiful this way. Just as you are beautiful unshaven and moving furniture."

"Then why have you avoided me?"

She missed a step and would have stumbled but for his firm hold on her. "I thought you were avoiding *me*. Ever since the second day, after your seasickness subsided. I thought you regretted what we did earlier. On the train."

His reply was instantaneous and adamant. "Never."

"But then why do you never touch me? Because an earl can't marry a girl like me and you're too good to want me for a mistress?"

He swore. "We were in such a confined space. Locked away from the world for fear that enemies might have followed us on board. That room has been our protection. I couldn't make advances, couldn't pressure you in any way. I won't be like Carsley or anyone of his ilk. I couldn't turn the safe haven of our room into a place where you were not wholly comfortable. I could never let you believe even for an instant that I might be anything other than your friend and champion."

She lifted her hand from his shoulder to his cheek. "My sweet, darling Nick. You can ask anything of me. At any time. I know you will never do anything I don't want."

His fingers tightened on hers. "And what do you want, Berries? I'll give you anything."

"You," she whispered, leaning into him, a breath away from that scandalous kiss. "I want you."

Nick's coat and tie hit the floor before the door lock had even clicked into place. Ida kicked off her dancing slippers and flung her gloves across the room, not caring where they landed. She could find them tomorrow.

She'd resisted kissing him until that very last waltz. By then the other gentlemen had all given up hope of wooing her and she had begun to hear mumbles of "Countess" and "Lady Sharpe." Which were better than the words they would say if they discovered she and Nick had been sharing a room in the guise of husband and wife.

Let them talk. Words couldn't touch her. She was already ruined at home. With no reputation left to protect, she could do as she pleased. And tonight she would have all that he would give her.

Nick's shoes went flying, followed by his waistcoat and shirt. Gracious, but the man could undress quickly! Ida gaped at him, fumbling with the tiny, hidden hooks in her bodice.

He paused with his hands on the fastenings of his trousers. "Is this too fast for you? Am I rushing you? I'm rushing you."

"No. I'm… distracted." Mesmerized. She couldn't take her eyes off his bare chest. She wanted to kiss him everywhere. And his lower half remained covered. Unacceptable. "Don't stop."

Ida found the last of the hooks and freed herself from the bodice. Nick's eyes darkened with hunger at the sight of her bared breasts. His tongue snaked out to moisten his lips.

"Sweet, luscious Berries. I'm going to eat you alive."

"Yes." She started in on her skirts. "Oh, please, Nick."

His trousers dropped to the floor. He cast stockings aside,

then drawers, leaving nothing but the man himself—strong, powerful, gorgeous, and hers for the taking.

Ida's skirts pooled at her feet. She stripped off her stockings as he watched, then shimmied out of the last of her underthings.

Her nakedness caused none of the embarrassment or shame people had implied it should. Only a fierce longing to have his body pressed to hers and a heady thrill at the obvious effect she had on him.

"What next?" she asked.

Nick stepped toward her, grasping her about the waist and drawing her into his powerful embrace.

"Now I worship you."

His mouth came down on hers and she gave herself up to the greedy joining of lips and savage thrusting of tongues. Tasting. Exploring. Devouring. Intoxicated by his wet, delicious heat.

Ida's skin prickled beneath the ceaseless roving of his hands. Up and down they flew, learning her every curve, savoring even the places she had believed imperfect. He kissed the pounding pulse at her throat, kneaded her buttocks, massaged her breasts, skillful fingers flicking at the stiff peaks of her nipples until she groaned his name and rocked her hips against him, aching to satisfy the pulsating need between her thighs.

His answering growl spurred her on. She curled her fingers around his rigid erection, stroking it from base to tip—perhaps the boldest, most spontaneous thing she had ever done.

"I want this." She stroked again, wrenching a strangled noise from his throat. "I want *you*. Please."

"God, Berries, yes. Yes to anything."

He extricated himself from her grip and lifted her up onto the bed, lowering his body onto hers. Her legs fell open instinctively, allowing him to settle between her thighs. She gasped when he nudged at her entrance.

"More?" he asked. "Or no?"

"Yes. Stop stopping." Her words gave way to a prolonged

sigh as he eased into her slick passage, stretching and filling her.

"Tell me if I hurt you," he murmured.

Ida responded with a thrust of her hips. "More. Keep going." Nick withdrew, then thrust deeper. She whimpered. "Yes, oh, yes."

"You slay me, Berries," he moaned. "I could die in the embrace of your sweet, honeyed quim."

"No. No dying. Only this. Only us."

Their bodies fell into a rhythm, rocking together, moving as one, pushing them nearer and nearer to the bliss of climax. She clutched at his shoulders, arching into him, every taut muscle straining for the coming release.

"Please. So close."

"Ida. God, Ida. My succulent Berries."

The crisis took her in a sudden rush, and she cried out, clawing at him as he thrust deep and hard, roaring his own satisfaction.

They collapsed together, rolling onto their sides. Ida snuggled against Nick's chest, stroking gentle caresses along his arm, basking in the contentment and joy of their union.

He pressed kisses into her hair, murmuring things she couldn't quite hear. Her eyes drifted closed, and she gave herself up to oblivion, lulled by the tenderness in his husky voice.

XXIII

The Best Laid Plans

"Ow."

Nick fished yet another hairpin from beneath the tangled sheets and tossed it into the growing pile on the bedside table. He pitied the maid who had to replace the bed linens in the morning and pick up all the pointy metal slivers they would surely leave behind. He spied a pin remaining in Ida's hair and gently worked it loose. That one, at least, wouldn't stab him while he snuggled her.

He toyed with her golden locks, so smooth and silky against his skin. God, but she was perfect. He must have had some rare stroke of luck to have found himself here, with such a woman in his arms. Nothing could have prepared him for the supreme bliss of bedding her or the soul-wrenching love that now flooded him in the aftermath. She didn't need him in any way, this woman of courage and passion. And yet she had given him the gift of herself. Freely, with no expectations. He owed her the world.

She shivered in her sleep and burrowed against him. Reluctantly, he tugged a blanket over her, hiding the body he could have gazed upon for hours at a time. He doused the oil lamp beside the bed and closed his eyes, content to let his other senses have their fill of her.

She smelled of sweat and sex and strawberries. It would be with him forever, this scent. He would go to his grave remembering it. The scent of her. The scent of happiness.

Next thing he knew, a rosy morning glow filled the cabin, and a new scent pricked at his nostrils. Dark, rich, bracing. His eyes snapped open. His arms were empty, the place beside him cold.

"Good morning," her cheery voice greeted him.

She had already dressed, he noted with disappointment, but the pot of coffee she had ordered for him almost made up for it. He crawled up out of the bed to pour himself a cup.

"Do you do this at home?" she asked, when he had settled himself at the table with his coffee and a sticky breakfast cake.

"Do what?"

"Have your coffee in the altogether."

Nick grinned and quirked an eyebrow. "You'll have to follow me home and find out."

Stormy desire swirled in her blue eyes, but she forced her gaze away from him and picked up the guidebook that lay on the table beside her empty teacup.

"That does sound appealing, but since we arrive in Bombay within the hour, I'm afraid we must first focus on work matters. Are you prepared for our arrival?"

"That depends. Am I an invading barbarian? If not, I had best finish my coffee and dress before I disembark."

"I was speaking of travel precautions, not your... nakedness." She waved a hand in his direction, carefully avoiding looking directly at him. "As I'm certain you are aware, various diseases are prevalent in tropical climates such as this, and we must take care to protect ourselves. Water ought to be boiled. Tea, coffee, and spirits are the safest drinks. Have you brought any medicines?"

"Medicines?" Nick echoed. "Just those in my coat pockets, but you know I don't drink potions."

"Mundane medicines are sufficient. Quinine to treat malaria, for instance. I have a supply, though I hope we shall not need it. One also ought to carry Cockle's Pills for indigestion and liver complaints, and…"

"What the deuce is a 'liver complaint'?"

"The book doesn't elaborate on that. It says only that one ought to have the pills. Along with Chlorodyne, which can be used to treat cough, consumption, fever, cholera and dysentery, epilepsy, hysteria, gout, toothache… Well, you get the idea."

"Indeed I do."

Quack medicine. He didn't even know of any potions that could cure such a wide array of complaints. Most potions against disease were far more specific. He wouldn't rule out the possibility of a cure-all, having experienced the effectiveness of the potion Ida had used on his knife wound. To date, though, he'd heard tell of no such thing.

"Oh, look at this." Ida lowered the book and pointed at an ad. "Invalid furniture and appliances. Perhaps we might invest in a wheeled chair to move you about during your bouts of seasickness."

"Are you mocking me, Miss Quimby?"

Her nose made a delightful little twitch when she smiled. "Perhaps a little. Now, the other problem we ought to concern ourselves with is the prevalence of insects. Recent scientific papers have demonstrated the ability of mosquitos to carry disease, and to that end I have developed a perfume of cedar, sage, cloves, and camphor to repel them. I suggest you spray a bit on your clothing as well as any uncovered skin."

"Ida," he sighed.

"Yes?"

"I know you are trying to protect me from any and all troubles, and I will be happy to use your anti-mosquito perfume, but in all honesty, I must say I'm far less concerned with disease than with the possibility of an attack. We have had no trouble on board this ship, and that concerns me. I fear someone may be lying in wait upon our arrival."

"Have you seen that thin-faced man?"

"No. But if he has hidden himself among the second class passengers we will have had little opportunity to encounter him."

"I haven't seen him, either. Nor the Holbecks."

"Who?"

"Your Fauxmericans? Their name is Holbeck. I find it unlikely they have merely disappeared, after all the attacks and warnings."

"Precisely. We must take steps to protect ourselves."

"I do have my knife, and you have the defensive potions. Do you think we ought to purchase additional weapons?"

Nick cringed. "I despise weapons and have no notion how to use them."

"Surely you can fence or shoot?"

"No."

A frown twisted her mouth. "I thought that was required knowledge for a gentleman."

He shrugged. "As you know from my stories, I wasn't the most masculine of boys, preferring tea parties to sport. My father was a scholar, so as long as I learned my Latin and Greek he didn't pressure me. I will watch tennis or cricket, but I don't play. And I have never touched a firearm. I'm fortunate in that my natural size and strength safeguarded me from the worst of the tauntings at school. I will fight to defend myself or another, but given the choice, I'd rather just sit down to tea."

"Or naked coffee."

He lifted his cup to her. "Only with you, my sweet."

Nick shifted to catch some of the breeze from Ida's fan. He drummed his fingers irritably on the desk while the man behind it puttered about, seemingly uninterested in the fact that he was neglecting paying customers. And this was supposed to be the best hotel in town?

Ida fanned harder. "Just think, when we left London we were shivering in our winter coats and now it is dreadfully hot."

Nick cleared his throat loudly. Again. The lobby was stifling. He couldn't wait to get to a room where he could open a window and let the breeze cool him. And perhaps strip both himself and Berries of all their clothing. Merely to cool off, of course.

The man turned around at last, eyeing Nick's coat with suspicion. He was bloody tired of that look. Perhaps it was time to retire the coat at last and have a new one made. Or maybe he wouldn't get a new one at all. He'd tell Ayleston he was quitting and then go back to redecorating his house. This time with a wife at his side. She'd need a brand new dressing room, her own study, and a place to craft her perfumes. He could suit the drawing room to her tastes.

"Can I help you?"

Nick's attention flew back to the jaded concierge behind the desk. "Yes. There should be a room for us under the name Masterson."

"One moment." He turned away, flipped through a book and shuffled a number of papers. After half a minute of this, he placed a stack of telegrams on the desk. "Here you are. These all came in for you yesterday evening."

Nick picked up the stack, scanning the top message. "Oh, for the love of…" He broke off before he could utter something inappropriate in public.

"What's wrong?" Ida asked.

"Nothing, except that my mother stubbornly refuses to understand the concept of telegrams. She's sent me a whole letter here, probably all in perfect, elegant sentences. 'My dearest Nicholas, I hope that this missive finds you well. I received the brief note you sent from Suez.' On and on. It must have cost a small fortune. At least she cares, I suppose." He glanced up at the concierge. "And our room key?"

The man began to thumb through papers again while Nick returned to his letter. He wanted to hear what his mother had to say about his intent to marry.

> *You sounded most adamant in your desire to marry Miss Quimby. I regret to inform you that you ought to reconsider such a match. The girl was involved in a terrible scandal two years ago and has not appeared in society since. I am surprised you did not know of it, as your friend Carsley was the jilted party. Miss Quimby is said to have humiliated him and made a spectacle of herself. She may be a fortune hunter, if her family has disowned her. Or she may be a title hunter, if she is anything like her parents. It certainly appears (even from your terse words) that she has already stolen your heart, but still I must caution you to guard yourself and be absolutely certain of who she is before you do anything foolish. I hope that this letter does not come too late. When you arrive home, if your wishes are unchanged, we can discuss the matter further. Until then, I remain, your loving mother, &c.*

"Damn right it's too late," he muttered. "Bring a pen and paper along with that key," he called to the concierge. "I need to write a telegram."

The man turned around. "I'm afraid we have no record of your room request, Mr. Masterson."

"What?" Nick's brows knit together. "I received a telegram telling me that my request had been received and the room would be waiting when I arrived." He dug through his pockets in search of papers, finding nothing. "I have it in my trunk, I believe."

The man behind the desk merely shrugged. "The paper will do you no good. We have no record of you and no other rooms available. You will have to go elsewhere."

Ida stepped up to the desk, closing her fan with an angry snap. "You would speak so rudely to a peer of the realm? Go back to those papers and look for a reservation for Lord Sharpe. If you don't have one, I would suggest you make one promptly, and deliver it with an apology."

Nick had to work to keep the scowl on his face. She would make a wonderful countess, his Berries. She was a natural leader, and the staid old blue-bloods could learn a thing or two from her.

The concierge remained unmoved. "I can tell you without looking again, Madam, that we have no such reservation."

That, at least, was the truth. Nick hadn't used his title since Paris, except for the fit of idiotic jealousy that had him throwing it around at Mr. Featherhead's ball.

"You had my mail," Nick said, keeping his voice stern, but even. "That is proof enough that I have ordered a room here, even without producing the papers that explicitly state that I not only ordered a room but received a confirmation of such from the management of this hotel. For an establishment that purports to be the finest in the city…"

"We *are* the finest in the city," the man interrupted. "Only the most distinguished of guests. Europeans only. You'll find no heathens or savages here, and certainly no…"

Nick spun around and stormed out, unwilling to listen to another hateful word. He'd sleep on the docks before letting that place have a single farthing. Ida jogged after him.

"What a horrid man. Better to go somewhere else. I will consult the guide for more options."

"There is another hotel down the street. We can send someone for our things once we have secured a room."

She dug into her satchel and flipped rapidly through her book. "I don't believe that hotel is listed here."

"Never mind that. It will do."

"But to go to a place that hasn't been at all recommended? After what a poor experience we have had with a hotel that *was* recommended?"

"It just goes to show that you can't trust those guidebooks."

She stopped in her tracks. "I planned my entire journey with my guidebooks. They helped me pack. They got me onboard all the correct trains and ships. They showed me hotels and restaurants that have all been excellent up until this one that *you* selected. I have found my way around foreign cities using only the provided maps, and learned the proper customs to avoid insulting the locals. My plans were *perfect* until you… you…"

"Ida." He cupped her face with both hands. "Ida, you're right. I'm sorry. I never meant to insult, only tease. Your guidebooks served you well. And your plans *were* perfect. You are amazing." He tucked a little unruly curl behind her ear. "Utterly amazing. I never stop thinking of you. I count the minutes when we are apart."

He froze. His thoughts snapped into alignment, like the hands of his watch hitting high noon. *Bloody fucking hell.*

Had he been treating her like a replacement for potions this entire time? Like some kind of *thing* that he craved? The balm for his addiction. The distraction from his troubles. He'd seized hold of her and refused to let go. No wonder he'd been such an impulsive arsehole. She deserved so much better.

"Nick?" Her hand lifted to cover his. "Is everything all right? You've gone a bit pale. Are you landsick now, after so long at sea? Because I will drag you to the hotel, if necessary. I've done it before, I can do it again."

The fierceness in her gaze sprung something loose in him. No. She was no mere thing to him. She was a woman, complex and unique. Soft curves and rock-hard strength. Full of cares and worries, fears and hopes—all things he wanted to share, as he wanted to share his own with her. He'd been stupid. Arrogant. Selfish. But he was learning. Bettering himself. Did he crave her? Certainly. But he also loved her. Trusted her. Respected her. He would leave their future in her hands. He would ask, but she would decide.

"No, I'm not sick. I'm in awe. I'm in love. I will never read your guidebooks, but I love how you love them. I love your plans. I love the tireless way you work to get everything just so. I love your attention to detail. I love the way you anticipate all possible problems to make the journey as safe and comfortable as possible. I love how you scold me for my own lax preparations. I love that when everything goes amok you pick yourself up, dust yourself off, and forge ahead with new plans, determined to make the best of everything. I love the way you have turned a tedious assignment into the best damn weeks of my life. I love you, Ida. I love you like a desert loves the rain. You are that rare, beautiful treasure bringing a burst of life and joy to this parched land."

He released her, though his body screamed for him to kiss her with everything he had. This road was too busy, however. Too public. He could hold out until they reached the privacy of a room.

"Nick," she gasped. She stared at him a long moment, her mouth agape, then placed a hand over his heart. The heat of her palm against his chest nearly undid his resolve.

"You are not a desert," she said. "You are a lush, wild jungle. Teeming with life and color."

"Hot," he breathed, relishing the color the word brought to her cheeks.

She licked her lips. "Moist."

"We need to go. Now."

He took her arm, and started down the street at a pace verging on indecorous. Only Ida's love of scanning the sights kept him from breaking into a run. She dragged him to a slow walk, pointing and chatting about the lush greenery giving way to crowded streets, the mix of Eastern and Western architecture, and the beautiful colors of the women's saris. When a monkey scampered past, a stolen bit of fruit in its paws, she squealed with delight, and Nick almost kissed her right there in the street. Again.

He was contemplating naughty things to whisper in her ear when she seized hold of his coat and hauled him behind a loaded wagon.

"Berries, what…?"

"Mr. Holbeck," she hissed. She peeked around the edge of the cart, then ducked back.

"Is he following us?"

"No. He looks to be headed toward the hotel we just left."

"Where he expects to find us."

"Exactly." She checked again. "I think you're right. I think we should take a room somewhere that's not in the guidebook."

"And under a different name. How would you feel if I were to become Mr. Quimby for the night?"

"That would be adorable, but too obvious. I suggest Creed."

"Who's Creed?"

"Her Majesty's favorite perfume house."

"Ah. And what happens when I forget my new name?"

"I'll do all the talking." She peeked around the wagon again. "Get ready to run, Mr. Creed. We are almost in the clear."

"Did I mention that I love the way you protect me?"

"Someone has to do for you what you do for others. I couldn't stand to lose you."

They raced together the rest of the way to the hotel. A few minutes of arrangements saw them locked safely in an elegantly appointed room. Ida settled herself into a chair, studying her map of the city and reviewing her notes. Nick sat on the edge of the bed, watching her, his body still tense, his mind racing. He both loved and hated the fearless way she strode into danger, refusing to let her enemies intimidate her. Soon she would set out to explore the town, purchase ingredients for her perfumes, and confront her ass of a brother. No one would stop her, though she knew enemies were lurking nearby.

He would do anything to protect her, but he was no warrior. All he had were a handful of potions and a certainty that he would die before letting harm come to her.

He prayed it would be enough.

XXIV

Villains and Heroes

"THAT'S EVERYTHING." Ida checked off the last item on her list. "We will drop these at the hotel and then go speak with my brother."

Nick nodded, taking up her package and adding it to the others he already carried. He'd been silent today, helping her tackle her chores with hardly a word, his eyes always searching for signs of danger. Always dedicated to both her goals and her safety. He was such a good man.

Her heart still hammered every time she thought of the way he had poured out his love to her. Was it possible, marriage between a nobleman and a scandal-ridden businesswoman? It was worth consideration, at least, because Ida suspected that this fierce desire to keep him always by her side might, in fact, be love.

They deposited Ida's purchases with the exceptionally kind and accommodating hotel staff and fortified themselves with a delicious, spicy luncheon before setting out for the Imperial Potions Company export warehouse and offices where Alfred worked. As she walked, she marveled again at how different life was here than at home. From the loose clothing and bare feet, to the way men and women carried loads balanced on their heads, to the pointed and scalloped arches framing doors and windows, everything seemed new and exciting to her. She had little time to explore, but she would treasure what time she had.

The midday sun shone bright and hot in the cloudless sky, and Ida tilted her parasol to shield herself from its scorching rays.

"I'm so pale," she said, as if anyone would fail to notice. "Part of me wants to hide inside from the sun, but this is such a beautiful country, full of color and tradition and interesting things I have never seen or experienced before."

Like the monkeys. She'd seen two more today, playing outside a small temple bursting with color and covered with statues of gods and goddesses she knew nothing about. Nick had needed to remind her the guidebook said monkeys were prone to biting. She'd promised not to take one home, no matter how adorable they were. Besides, she'd already collected an earl on this journey. She had enough primates for one excursion.

"I love that I have been able to visit," Ida went on, "and I do wish I had more time for sightseeing, but I would never be able to stay. I'm not at all fit for the climate. Though many Englishmen are able to adapt, I suppose." She gestured at a cluster of British soldiers walking in the opposite direction, their tanned faces suggesting they'd been in India a good long while.

"We shouldn't be here," Nick replied.

"Because I'm not suited to the sun? Or are you still worried about an attack? I'm trying to remain vigilant."

"I mean we British shouldn't be here. What gave us the right to claim this land for our empire? It belonged to someone else. It belongs to the people here."

Ida gaped up at him. "You are an anti-colonialist!"

He gave an awkward cough. "I may have made myself infamous in Parliament by ranting to that effect once."

"Of course you did!" She laughed.

"They laughed at me, too. But unlike you, they laughed because they thought I was off my head."

"My poor Nick. You cannot be what the world expects, can you?"

"Nor can you." The smile he gave her was full of warmth. "Perhaps that is why we are drawn to one another."

She fluttered her eyelashes at him. "And here I thought you simply liked the color pink."

"I do now. I love it, in fact."

"Then there is something you must know before it's too late."

His eyes took on a wicked gleam as they ran up and down her body. "I believe it is already too late, love."

Ida looked down at the ground, pretending shame. "Nick, I'm so sorry, but some of the dresses in my wardrobe at home are other colors."

"Dammit, Ida, then how am I supposed to match you to the curtains?"

She looked up into his sparkling eyes and they laughed together, fingers interlacing as they walked on, hand-in-hand.

The realization that this was to be her life struck her square in the chest. It filled her with joy, this sense of affection and camaraderie, of knowing when to tease and when to comfort—this intimacy not just of body but of mind. She liked him, respected him, desired him. Loved him. They would share a bed and a home, encourage one another's hopes and dreams, build a family together. He would be her Mr. Masterson, and she would be his Lady Sharpe.

And her good-for-nothing brother was about to be the first in the family to meet her soon-to-be-husband.

She rapped on Alfred's door, a tired-looking slab of oak at the end of a dark hall in an unimpressive building, with rusty hinges and a tarnished plaque stating, "Mr. A. Quimby."

The door groaned as it opened and Alfred's head poked

out, his bushy, blond whiskers thicker and wilder than when she'd seen him last. His blue eyes grew wide with horror.

"Ida!"

She stuck her parasol into the doorway to prevent him from closing it, and pushed her way inside.

"You shouldn't be here," he protested. "I told you not to come. I warned you repeatedly."

"Oh?" A more astute man might have shied away from the icy fury in her tone, but Alfred had never been one to notice the moods of others. "Are you telling me that *you* are the one responsible for the bullet lodged outside our train compartment? Or the knife stabbed into my pillow?"

"No! I… Did those things really happen?"

Nick stepped up beside Ida, his towering form seeming to fill all the empty space in the small office.

"They most certainly did," he replied, his deep voice devoid of all emotion.

Alfred stared at Nick. "Good God, Ida, did you hire a bodyguard?"

"I am no bodyguard, Mr. Quimby. My name is Nicholas Masterson, Earl of Sharpe and Miss Quimby's traveling companion, and I suggest you begin with an apology and finish by giving the lady what's she's come for."

Alfred's eyes swung back to Ida. "Traveling companion? You've become some gentleman's doxy? I guess all those things everyone said about you—"

"Shut your mouth." Nick backed Alfred into the desk, his hands balling into fists. "I abhor violence, but I will break your nose if you utter one more—" He froze, his gaze dropping to stare at the ledgerbook on the desk. "Well, isn't that interesting?"

"No!" Alfred lunged for the book, but Nick pushed him aside and circled the desk for a better look.

"Mr. Quimby, I suggest you discuss the terms of your agreement with your sister while I make a few notes."

"Oh, Alfred, what have you done?" Ida sighed.

"Nothing! I have a job! I record the shipments, nothing more!"

She eyed the paper beside the ledgerbook, its neat columns of figures matching those on the open page of the book. Or nearly.

"You are falsifying the records!"

"And destroying the evidence." Nick gestured at the fire burning low in the hearth. Wisps of ash that may once have been papers dusted the coals. "Or is it simply not hot enough for you today?" He withdrew a clean sheet of paper from a desk drawer and began to copy down the numbers.

"Everything there is as it should be," Alfred protested weakly.

"Hmm," Ida replied. "More serum arriving from the sources than is shipped out. Where is the extra going? Some secret stash?"

"No! There isn't… I don't know. I only list what is true."

"Then why are you changing the numbers? Are you saying that serum is simply disappearing between the sources and this facility?"

"The sources are far to the south. One in Ceylon and another near Mysore. It's a long journey. Anything can happen. There is criminal activity."

Nick glanced up from his writing. "Then why is there no potions black market? Excuse me if I don't believe the criminals here are so stupid they would destroy a valuable commodity rather than selling it."

"I-it's true."

"Also, if I'm not mistaken, the amounts per bottle listed here are higher by half an ounce than what customers are receiving in Europe."

"T-the contents settle during shipment."

"Oh, for goodness' sake, Alfred," Ida said, "You are such a cabbagehead. You boast of your important work, but you're no more than a lackey. You do whatever your superiors tell you, thinking it will raise your standing with them. It won't. They're using you, and if anyone exposes their crimes, you'll take the fall."

"There is no crime. The serum is r-running out. I swear."

"It seems to me that someone is manufacturing an artificial shortage to drive up prices."

"You're wrong." Alfred tried to snatch the papers again but Nick yanked them out of his reach. "Can't you make him stop?"

"And why should I? You deserve nothing from me, after all your horrid threats. I could have been killed!"

"I told you, I didn't do those things! I only sent a few telegrams. Lord Holbeck said he'd scare you off. He must have done it."

"Oh, that's so much better. It wasn't you. It was only your friend."

Alfred shrugged, not seeming to grasp the sarcasm.

"What does he want with me?"

"He's just one of those impoverished lords, looking for a money-making scheme. I sold him your potion perfume idea, but I didn't think he'd attack you!"

"You sold him my idea?" Ida surged toward him, her hands shaking with rage. "You. Sold. My. Idea."

Alfred stumbled backward. "N-no offense, Ida, but you're just a woman. What do you know about business?"

Ida's palm cracked him hard across the face. "I take a great deal of offense you… you… Nick, help me."

"Dimwitted, misogynistic fuck-beggar?" he offered.

"Yes. That." She pushed her brother backwards until he plopped down onto the dilapidated chair meant for the visitors he probably never had. "Now you listen to me, Alfred Quimby. I have a business that I started and that I intend to keep, and no one is going to stop me. Not Mother and Father, not Holbeck, not you. You promised me. You owe me. You told me you could get me serum, and that is precisely what you are going to do."

Ida lifted her skirt—causing Alfred to yelp in horror—and unfastened the tiny purse tied to her petticoat. She withdrew two carefully folded banknotes and dropped them in her brother's lap.

"There. That was the price you quoted me. I expect two cases of serum to await me at the Grand Western Hotel first thing in the morning. The cases will be full and each bottle will contain the correct amount of undiluted liquid. Mr. Masterson is a potions specialist, and he will be able to tell if you have cheated me."

"But, Ida, I can't—"

"You *will*. I don't care how much it costs you or how difficult it is to obtain. We had an agreement, and you will abide by it. Because your other option is that I turn you over to the authorities for fraud."

"That's blackmail!"

"You sold my business idea to people who want to murder me. I think this a rather soft punishment, all things considered."

She glared at him until his eyes dropped to the floor. "All right, Ida. I'll get you the serum. Please, just go away. And take your nosy, hulking protector with you."

Nick folded his paper and tucked it into a pocket. "I'm done here. Shall we go, my dear?"

"Yes, let's. I find that the sight of my horrid brother is making me rather queasy." She began to follow Nick out into the hall, then paused and ducked back into the office for a last word. "Oh, and Alfred, you are not invited to the wedding."

"What wedding?"

"Mine, of course. To Mr. Masterson."

"He'll never offer for you, Ida. Not if he's really a lord."

"Well, if he doesn't propose, I will. Good day." She spun away and closed the door firmly behind her.

Back outdoors, Ida again put up her parasol and took hold of Nick's hand. Her happy mood had been squelched, but she'd finished the task she'd set herself. Alfred would do as she asked. He was terrified of prison. She suspected he'd flee home to England before long and find himself a new job licking the boots of some other corrupt employer.

The street was oddly deserted. True, it was dreadfully hot, but the lack of people anywhere surprised Ida. Perhaps in this area of British-run warehouses and offices, everyone remained indoors during the heat of the afternoon.

"That's quite far enough, Miss Quimby."

Ida and Nick spun as one. Lord Holbeck stood a few feet away, a heavy revolver in his hand. His wife, garbed in a dress the same shade of pink as Ida's, toyed with a gleaming gold knife. She smiled sweetly.

"Such a pleasure to see you again, Miss Quimby," she cooed. "You really should have heeded our warnings, however. My husband is dreadfully out-of-sorts, as you can see."

Lord Holbeck leveled his gun at Ida, gesturing for her to step into the narrow alley next to Alfred's building. Nick leapt in front of her, but she slipped out from behind him, snapping her parasol closed and brandishing it like a club.

Lady Holbeck laughed. "You are so fierce, Miss Quimby. How utterly charming. No wonder you weren't scared off by silly things like gunfire and steak knives. I think perhaps we could have been friends under different circumstances."

"You mean if you weren't an evil, business-stealing, murderous harpy?"

Nick reached inside his coat, but Lord Holbeck swung the pistol to aim straight for his heart.

"Hands where I can see them, Sharpe," he barked. "I've heard about you and your love of potions, and I won't have you using any of them on me. Now get into that alley before anyone happens along and sees us."

"We'll take it from here," a new voice rang out. The thin-faced man materialized from somewhere down the alley, flanked by two men easily as tall as Nick, with bulging arms and necks as thick as tree trunks.

"What the devil?" Holbeck exclaimed.

"I have a prior claim on the earl, here," Thin-Face said. His high, monotone voice sent a chill down Ida's spine. "You can have the girl."

"He knows too much," Holbeck spat. "He could ruin my business."

"*My* business, darling," Lady Holbeck replied, sidling up to him. "You wouldn't know a perfume if it hit you in the face."

"Shut your trap, wench. Can't you see—"

Lady Holbeck plunged her knife into his gut and his words became a scream. She gave the blade a vicious twist before yanking it free.

"Oh, dear. It seems my husband has been set upon by ruffians. Such a dangerous, uncivilized place, this."

Ida looked away from Holbeck's crumpled, whimpering form, bile rising in her throat. Her grip tightened on her parasol. She wouldn't let herself or Nick suffer the same fate.

"Run, Ida," Nick whispered. "I'll hold them off until you get away."

She pressed closer to him. "No."

"Please, Ida."

"The girl is yours, Lady Holbeck," Thin-Face said. "We'll handle Lord Sharpe." He snapped his fingers, and the two thugs sprang at Nick, grabbing him and hauling him away as he struggled to break free.

"No!" Ida screamed.

Lady Holbeck darted forward, and Ida swung the parasol to keep her at arms' length.

"Help!"

Footsteps echoed in the distance. The road couldn't remain empty for long in such a bustling city. Someone would hear her.

"Help!" she shouted again.

"Run, Ida!" Nick shouted. One of the thugs landed a punch to his gut and Nick grunted and doubled over. He responded with an elbow to the man's ribs. "Run," he gasped. "You're faster than she is."

Ida swung at Lady Holbeck again, catching the brim of her wide hat and sending it flying. "I won't leave you!"

The footsteps came nearer, and a trio of redcoats turned off a side street, their swords drawn.

"Help us!" Ida screamed, putting all the air she had behind her words. "We're under attack!"

She and Lady Holbeck circled one another as the soldiers came running over. The men stopped several yards away, surveying the scene.

"See that the chit with the parasol doesn't run away," Thin-Face barked instructions. The soldiers nodded and spread out to block any path of escape.

"What?" Fueled with new fury, Ida landed a blow to Lady Holbeck's arm that drew a yelp of pain. "You traitorous blackguards! I am a citizen of Her Majesty's Empire, and he is a peer of the realm! How dare you stand there and...*eep!*" She darted out of the reach of the knife. "And just watch us struggle!"

One of the thugs grappling with Nick collapsed, the sleeping potion syringe jutting from his arm. The second stumbled backwards, clawing at his face before slumping to the ground. Nick whirled to face Ida, shouting her name, the stun potion clutched in his hand. Blood ran down the side of his face, and he winced as he limped toward her.

"You fools," Thin-Face snarled. "Didn't you hear the man say not to let him reach inside his coat?" He snapped his fingers at the soldiers. "Get him."

The trio converged on Nick, forming a circle around him. One of them flicked his sword, and the stun potion went flying. Nick cried out and clutched his hand.

"Nick!"

Ida kicked at Lady Holbeck, catching her in the shin before bringing the parasol down on her right shoulder. Lady Holbeck staggered, but neither fell nor lost her grip on the knife. She backed off, regrouping, regarding Ida with that vicious-sweet smile.

"Don't worry, dear, you'll be dead soon, so what does it matter if they kill your lover?"

Ida shuffled toward the middle of the street, trying to stay where she could see Nick. Somehow she needed to get past Lady Holbeck if she were to have any chance to save him.

"Don't let him reach into that coat," Thin-Face warned the soldiers.

The soldiers pressed closer. Nick jammed his hands into his outer pockets, coming up with nothing more than a few coins, the receipts from Ida's morning purchases, and Anna the boy rabbit. Ida's heart threatened to pound out of her chest. Without his potions he was defenseless. The soldier behind Nick slashed at him, splitting open both the frock coat and the waistcoat beneath. A spot of blood bloomed on Nick's white shirt.

"No!"

Ida ran toward him, thinking of nothing except reaching him before one of those swords went straight through his heart. Lady Holbeck lunged, and Ida only had time to twist and duck as the golden blade sliced through the air. The knife caught in her hair, wrenching it painfully, but she jerked herself free, at the same time thrusting the parasol at Lady Holbeck's unprotected groin. The tip of the parasol speared Lady Holbeck directly in her lady parts, and she crumpled. Ida swung her makeshift weapon one last time, bringing it down on her enemy's head. The parasol cracked in two, but Lady Holbeck fell still and silent.

"Run, Ida!" Nick's cry was fraught with pain. He had dropped to the ground and was huddled in a ball, protecting his head and belly from the heavy boots of the soldiers. His ruined coat had been torn from his back and the scraps lay strewn about the street, the potions out-of-reach and useless. "Run, Ida, please!"

Ida ran. Straight for the part of the coat that held the healing potions. Thin-Face saw her coming, and grabbed for her, but she dove to the ground, leaving him grasping at empty air. Her fingers had just curled around the two tiny bottles when she heard the unmistakable pop of a cork.

The world exploded.

XXV

To Your Health

"Berries?"

The question rasped out of him in barely a whisper. Nick couldn't make sense of anything through the throbbing in his head. Why was she shouting at him from so far away? And what was making that damned annoying ringing noise?

"Nick!" she cried again, her voice high and hysterical. "Oh, please, Nick."

Not distant. Muted. The ringing came from inside his own ears.

"Please, don't be dead. Please."

Dead? Why would he be…

Everything crashed in on him at once. The attack. His desperation. The little toy clutched in his hand, innocent vessel of the most barbaric of weapons.

His eyes flew open in terror.

"Ida!" The force of the scream burned his lungs. "Ida, stay down!"

He tried to turn around, but the movement sent pain spiraling through every limb. Stars danced in front of his eyes, obscuring the blue-gray smoke that radiated upward and outward in a ring of torment. Where was she? Oh, God, where was she? If she breathed in even a single lungful of that poison, it would end him.

He screamed her name again, forcing his head to turn through the stabs of agony. No more than a yard away lay one of the men who had beaten him, gibbering unintelligibly and flailing at demons that didn't exist. Why hadn't she run?

"Nick." Her voice was soft now, and so close.

He wrenched himself around, all the pain vanishing at the sight of her crawling to him, her head ducked well below the toxic smoke and further protected beneath a large scrap of his ruined coat. Her hand settled on his arm and she nuzzled against his shoulder.

"You're alive," she sobbed. "I was s-so scared. Please don't leave me. I need you so much."

She needed him? Impossible. His sweet, little Berries was as strong as twenty men together. He was the one in need. He was weak. But now that she was at his side, alive and well, he thought perhaps he could do anything. He would fly if she asked it of him.

"Drink this."

Nick recoiled from the potion. *Anything but that.*

"Nick, you must." Her free hand lifted to his cheek, stroking him but for a moment before withdrawing. Blood coated her elegant fingers. "You are bleeding. You are broken. You must drink the potion. I won't lose you."

She held the small bottle to his lips. His nostrils flared at the familiar hint of spice and magic. Serum. Sharp and potent. The craving wound its way through him, setting his pulse to racing and his limbs to trembling. He crushed her hand beneath his, not knowing whether he meant to push the potion away or claim it as his own.

"Will you help me, Berries? When the cravings grow worse, when I beg for more, will you help me?"

"Yes. Anything. Everything you need. I love you, Nick. I love you and if you bleed out here in the street it will shatter my heart."

She tilted the bottle against his lips. Nick opened his mouth and drank the contents down, licking up even the drops that dribbled down his chin.

God, what a sensation. The potion burned and soothed. Heated and cooled. The throbbing in his head stilled. The ringing in his ears subsided. His pain faded into a series of distant aches, his lacerated flesh tingling as the wounds began to knit together. Nick's head swam from the delicious power of it.

"More," he gasped. "Give me the other one."

"No."

He snatched at the bottle she held just out of reach. "I need it."

"Not yet. One may be enough." She pulled her skirt aside and tucked the remaining potion into her purse.

"I'll strip that dress off you and have both you and the potion," he vowed.

"You'll have what I say you can have," she snapped.

Nick's mouth opened and closed. She spoke the absolute truth, and he had no reply. He could do nothing but lie there and beg, his mind a muddle, consumed by desperate wanting.

"Zero days," he sighed. "Zero hours, zero minutes."

Ida traced his jawline with a single finger, then pressed it to his lips. "Be strong, my love. I'm here to help, just as I promised."

"Berries." He clasped her hand, kissing it, unwilling to part from the taste of her. "I'm not certain which I want more, you or that potion."

"A good sign that your body is healing. We can save the potion. In case of another attack."

Only the slight tremble of her lower lip betrayed her fear. So brave. His stalwart protector.

"You," he said. "Definitely you."

"We should go, if you are able to walk."

Nick grabbed her before she could sit up. "No!" He hauled her against his chest. "Stay down until all the smoke has dissipated. It's poison."

Wide-eyed, she scanned the fading blue haze. "The smoke killed those men? Not the explosion?"

"They're not dead." He pushed up just enough to glance at his fallen enemies. Only Thin-Face was twitching. A plaintive whimper rose from one of the still bodies.

"Dying, then."

"No." He looked away, fighting the nausea building in his stomach. "Their bodies are likely to recover, but their minds are shattered. They are prisoners within their own brains, sightless but for mad hallucinations, forever haunted by terrors of their own devising."

Ida gasped in horror. She grabbed the remnant of his coat and flung it over both their heads.

"We're safe enough here, low and in the center," Nick said, pushing away the worthless scrap of material. "The explosion pushed the smoke out and up, and it weakens over time. Ten, fifteen minutes and the air will be clear again."

"Why didn't you tell me you had such a weapon?"

"I hoped never to use it. It sickens me, what I've done. Yet I would do it again, to save myself. To save you. Us."

"How did you do it? They had stripped you of all your potions."

"No, they hadn't." Nick picked up Anna the rabbit, setting him where Ida could see. The little toy looked tired now, with his tail missing and his belly deflated. A warrior, victorious through sacrifice. "I told you he reminded me of my sister. Small, but fierce. The secret weapon idea was something we concocted during a childhood game. Now I will refill him with proper stuffing and pin a medal to his chest. For saving our future. He will accompany us everywhere."

"Oh, Nick." She wrapped her arms around him, and they held one another in silence until the air had cleared and people began to filter into the street.

He sat up, testing his arms and legs. A bit of soreness lingered, but everything worked, and he wasn't bleeding anywhere.

"We had best be on our way," he said. "Thin-Face must have devised some roadblock to keep people away while he did his dirty deed, but it appears to be failing, and there will be questions about the dead man and the mad soldiers."

"Yes. I think it best we return to the hotel and prepare to head for home as soon as possible."

Ida climbed to her feet, shaking out her skirts. She reached up to adjust her hair, and a thick clump of blond locks fell away, landing in a heap at her feet.

"My hair! That woman!" She whirled around, jarring more bits of hair loose, her gaze coming to rest on her broken parasol. "And she's gone! She got away, that stupid, stabby harpy!" Ida burst into tears. "And n-now I'm s-sobbing over something as unimportant as hair."

Nick scooped up the cut-off locks of hair, then put an arm around her, leading her down the street. "I may join you in that. Not only did I lose my coat, but one of the bastards did this." He showed her his pocket watch, the glass cracked, the hands frozen. "I don't know how long it's been since I last drank a potion." His voice broke on the last word. "Seems a trivial concern after such an ordeal."

Ida wiped at her watery eyes. "It's not. And you don't need to know the exact time. Any amount of time is positive. Besides, there were no potions on the steamer to Bombay. None."

"A fact I will be noting in my report to my uncle."

"It stands to reason there will be no potions on the return ship. You will have two weeks free from temptation. We will depart tomorrow, as soon as I have my serum. Which I vow not to let you drink. I will hide it, if necessary." She paused. "You don't mind, do you? Leaving, I mean? I'm sure there is more we could learn about the serum shortage."

"Let someone else determine whether there are really criminals hijacking supply lines or some scheming company man creating a secret stash. Plotters like Thin-Face, mercenary thugs bigger than me, and traitorous British soldiers? I'm not equipped to handle those things, and I only have one Anna the rabbit. Let them send a professional. I want to go home. I have plans to take a wife and settle down."

Her blue eyes fixed on his, staring down into his very soul. "I'd like to hear these plans of yours."

His grip on her tightened. "You will, love. Soon."

"Soon" was delayed, of course, by his need to send several telegrams and procure an appropriate ring, followed by the inevitable day and a half of seasickness that accompanied their hasty departure. All of which led to him pacing the deck on their second afternoon at sea, muttering to himself like a madman and asking every passerby for the time. God, but he missed his watch.

His heart skipped a beat when he caught sight of her pink dress. A silk scarf she'd purchased in India covered her head, now that she had neither hat nor parasol. He'd buy her fifty of each when they were back in London, if it pleased her. She hurried across the deck to him, her fingers holding the scarf tight against the wind, an uncertain frown on her face.

"Well, the only barber on the ship specializes in men's haircuts, naturally," she said. "He was properly horrified by what had happened to my hair, though, and he worked very hard to make me presentable." She tugged the scarf away. "What do you think?"

Nick's jaw dropped. Waves of flaxen hair fell just to her chin, a few shorter locks curling down across her forehead. This new, short style tumbled free of any pins or pomades, framing her face, accentuating the roundness of her cheeks and the elfin point to her chin. It was bouncy, light, and perfectly Ida. He loved it.

"I hope you paid him well, because you look absolutely adorable."

Her eyes lit up. "I'm so glad! I thought I might be the only person in the world to like it."

"Even if you were, that's all that matters, now isn't it?"

"That is true, I suppose, but I did want you to like it, too. I know you like to play with my hair."

What he liked was that amorous gleam in her eyes. Last night he'd been too ill to do more than hold her hand. He would make up for it tonight, in celebration of their approaching nuptials.

"I expect I will continue to play with your hair regardless of how you may style it. And now I have this." He unbuttoned his cuff and pulled up his sleeve enough to display the bracelet he'd woven from her shorn-off tresses. "So I have a piece of you with me at all times."

"Is that what you were fidgeting with while I was reading to you last night?"

"I was too sick to do much else. It was soothing."

"You're so sweet."

Nick's heart swelled every time she said that. Sweet. It wasn't a manly sort of compliment. Most people remarked on his height or his strength. Some women called him handsome. Ida liked those things, certainly, but most of all she loved his heart. The heart she would own for all time.

"I have something important to discuss with you, Berries."

"Yes." She stepped closer, holding out both hands.

Nick curled his fingers around hers and sank to one knee.

"My darling Miss Quimby. Even before I knew your name, I knew you were the woman for me. I knew it from your smile and your laugh. From your stalwart heart and your unending kindness. You slay me with your wit and vanquish me with your love. You are sunshine and moonlight, lighting my path, brightening my days and my nights. There is no one I want more in my life than you, my sweet Berries. Please, my love, won't you propose to me?"

"What?"

Nick wanted to kiss the little crinkle of confusion at the top of her nose.

"I overheard what you said to your brother, and I realized that I desperately wanted to hear how you would propose to me. Won't you, please?"

The corner of her lips twitched, growing slowly into a smile that brought a glow to her entire face.

"Very well. I adore you, Nicholas Masterson, Earl of Sharpe. I love your unconventional habits and your generous heart. You don't simply care for me. You respect me. You trust me. You desire me as I am. It means so much to me, to be truly loved and valued. And since I love you even despite your aristocratic tendency toward imperious decision-making, I think I have no choice but to marry you. Will you become my true, legal husband? Will you live with me not only on a boat or a train, but in a home of our own? Will you be my traveling companion for the whole journey of my life?"

Nick pulled her against him, pillowing his head against her soft breasts. "Yes, Ida. God, yes. Forever, yes."

He dug the ring out of his pocket and slid it onto her finger. The pink, heart-shaped stone was probably only glass, but he didn't care and he knew she wouldn't either. She beamed down at it and kissed his brow.

"I know the honeymoon is supposed to happen after the wedding," she said, "but since we are traveling already, I have a few places I should like to go on our way home. First, I think we should take a different route through Italy to visit Venice. Then, I would like to spend some time in Grasse for more perfume study. A few more days in Paris would not be amiss, either."

Nick stood up, swept her off her feet and kissed her soundly before setting her back down.

"Plan away, my Berries, plan away. I will follow wherever you go."

XXVI

Bath, Interrupted

London, one month later

A PERFECTLY MANICURED HAND caught the bathing chamber door an instant before it closed. Ida tugged her dressing gown back into place as her mother swept into the room. She looked longingly at the massive, built-in tub, tendrils of steam rising from its clean, hot water. It was too much to ask, it seemed, to have a chance to wash and relax before her family confronted her.

"Ida, darling!" Her mother's exuberant voice reverberated off the tiles. She held her arms out for an embrace.

Ida accepted the hug, her nose twitching as she tried to hide her frown. Well, this was unexpected. She couldn't remember the last time anyone in the family had seemed genuinely pleased with her.

"It's good to see you, Mama."

"Yes, yes." Lady Quimby stepped back and checked her clothing for wrinkles. "But, darling, you simply must explain yourself. You vanish with nothing more than a note stating that you are going out of the country, and then one Sunday we are sitting in church and what do we hear? This!" She waved a piece of paper in Ida's face. "Banns of marriage. Between who, might you ask? The Earl of Sharpe and Miss Ida Quimby! We were certain it must be a mistake or a prank by one of your brothers, but then there it was again the next Sunday, and the one after. All without a word from you. What do you have to say for yourself?"

"Um… Yes, I am engaged to Lord Sharpe."

Who would be given a piece of Ida's mind the moment she next saw him. He had arranged to have the banns posted without her knowledge? He had to have sent a message home before they'd left India. Which meant *before* they had become engaged.

"Even if he is an arrogant, high-handed—" she muttered.

"An earl! Oh, Ida!" Her mother hugged her again, so forcefully that she nearly toppled both of them into the bathtub.

Where the water was losing its luxurious heat with every second they wasted.

"Yes, Mama. Might we perhaps talk more after I have bathed?"

Lady Quimby spared only a momentary glance at the tub. "Yes, yes, but *how* did you manage to catch him? I thought all hope was lost after that scandal." She scanned Ida head to toe. Ida clutched her robe tighter beneath the scrutiny. "Are you increasing?"

"What?" In her shock, Ida lost her hold on her dressing gown and it gaped open nearly to her navel. "No!"

At least she hadn't been as of two weeks ago. She couldn't say what might have happened since. Given the frequency of their intimacies, they were bound to have a child sooner or later.

"You cannot blame me for thinking it. Your reputation is stained, and no noble family desires that sort of notoriety. But Sharpe is said to be an honorable man, so I'm certain he would do the right thing by a woman carrying his child."

Ida put her hands on her hips, her robe slipping even further to fully expose one breast. She stopped herself from reaching to cover it. Perhaps if she were naked her mother would let her get on with her bath.

"I did *not* seduce him into marriage. He loves me. Now may I *please*—"

The door flew open again to admit a young housemaid with red cheeks and trembling hands.

"I'm s-so sorry, m-my lady." The girl shook so hard she could hardly get her words out. "But t-there is a man in Miss Ida's b-bedchamber, going through all her clothing and u-using funny words like sir-rule-something."

"Cerulean. It's a shade of blue." Nick's voice sent a shiver of pleasure through Ida even before he filled the doorway. "The color of Miss Quimby's eyes."

"You're here," she blurted. "So soon?"

He hadn't changed out of his travel clothing. Had he not gone home at all? He had promised to come by to speak with her father and help her select a wedding dress, but she'd thought he'd meant tomorrow. At the very least, she had anticipated having the time to bathe. It was as if everyone in her life had conspired to keep her out of that tub. The heat of the water warmed her backside, taunting her.

Ida's mother shrieked before Nick could reply. "How dare you intrude upon my daughter in such a fashion! Can you not see that this is a bathing chamber and she is in a state of dishabille!"

Ida readjusted her dressing gown, but not before she caught the twinkle in his amber eyes. Anticipation. Desire. And not a little mischief.

"I can, indeed," Nick said. "However, it seemed ungentlemanly to remark upon it."

Lady Quimby brushed past the still-quivering maid and grabbed hold of Nick's lapels. Few people, Ida imagined, would dare touch an earl in such a fashion. Any who did would push him out of the room. Her mother pulled him further inside.

"You have thoroughly compromised her with your boorish behavior! I insist that you marry her!"

Nick extricated himself from Lady Quimby's grip and gave her a winning smile. "Excellent. How does tomorrow work for you?"

"Tomorrow?" Ida squeaked.

Her mother stormed from the room, pushing the poor chambermaid in front of her. "Sir Mortimer will be hearing about this!" She yanked the door closed and a moment later Ida heard the click of a turning key.

For several seconds, Nick and Ida stared together at the closed door.

"I do believe your mother has just locked me in this bathing chamber with you."

"She is a rather determined sort of woman."

A twitch at the corner of Nick's mouth betrayed his amusement. "I don't know anyone like that."

"Yes, well, unfortunately we are often at odds. As you can no doubt tell, she very much wishes for me to marry well. She was devastated when I refused all the fortune hunters after the scandal. And I don't think she really believes that you want to marry me. Now, if you will excuse me, I would like to take my bath." Ida shucked her robe and stepped into the tub.

Nick shrugged out of his coat. "Would you care for some company?"

A quiver of excitement raced through her disloyal body. Much as she longed for his hands on her skin, she wouldn't let him near until she had spoken her piece.

"Oh, no. Not just yet. You have some explaining to do."

His fingers stilled on the buttons of his waistcoat. "I meant to go home. I started to go home. I made my driver stop and let me out. I realized that I didn't want to live apart from you. Not even for a day."

"That's very romantic, and I don't mind that you are here, or even that you already started looking for a wedding dress."

"The cerulean silk with the pale pink lace overlay. I like the elegance and the small bustle that will show off your bum."

"Oh, that will be perfect. I love that dress and haven't yet had an occasion to wear it. But you are distracting me from the point."

Nick's gaze followed the bar of soap as Ida ran it along her arm. "You are distracting me, as well."

"You posted the banns without telling me."

"True."

"And you did it before we were officially engaged?"

"To be fair, you had already informed your brother that you intended to marry me. I wouldn't have done it otherwise. I wanted to be expeditious. I wasn't joking about tomorrow, Ida. I want to marry you as soon as possible. I want us to be permanent. I want the world to know." He bent to retrieve his coat. "Which is no excuse for not telling you. I had a month to do so. I apologize, and I will go pound on the door until someone lets me out so you might be left in peace."

"No."

The coat slipped from his fingers. "You would prefer I stay?"

"Yes. Join me."

Even after all their time together, Ida still marveled at how quickly Nick could undress himself. Not one minute passed by before he was sliding into the tub beside her.

"I will install a bath like this in our house," he promised, taking the soap from her hand and sliding it over her neck and chest. "I will hire a contractor at once."

"Mmm," Ida replied, less interested in his plans than in his attention to scrubbing her breasts perfectly clean.

"Different tile, though," he murmured. "This looks like a garish Roman bathhouse."

"My father has flamboyant tastes." She snagged a washcloth and dragged it slowly along Nick's muscled thigh.

"Indeed. But he raised the finest of daughters, so I will forgive him his foibles and instead admire his intelligence and hard work."

Ida's hand froze inches from her target, her amorous intentions momentarily forgotten. "You don't hate my family?"

"We are all flawed, Berries. I would be the worst sort of hypocrite to expect perfection of anyone. Your parents didn't cast you out after your scandal or force you to wed where you did not wish. They may be self-absorbed and they don't understand you at all, but they aren't cruel. And I think they do love you, albeit in a somewhat misguided fashion."

"I think so, too. They will love you, as well, once they get to know you. Now they love your money and your title, but when they see you for who you are it will become more than that. They will love you for accepting them when so many do not. I love you for accepting them."

He dropped a soft kiss on her lips. "How could I not, when you accept me and all my oddities and weaknesses?" The soap slipped from his hand as he pulled her into a fierce embrace. "My darling, lovely, bride-to-be."

Ida threaded her fingers through his hair and kissed him fervently, sucking hard on his bottom lip and thrusting her tongue to meet his. Nick groaned and dragged her atop him, lifting her half out of the water. The rush of cool air drew her nipples to taut peaks and he teased them with gentle flicks of his warm fingers.

Ida delved for the soap, groping about in the water until her fingers found the slippery, floral-scented bar. She scrubbed across Nick's chest, over his own hardened nipples, and down his belly.

"You are a dirty, dirty man," she murmured.

"Filthy," he agreed, sliding his hands lower to fondle her buttocks.

Ida continued downward, running her soap through the curly, dark hairs that surrounded his sex. "You require vigorous washing." She slid the bar over his cock, from the base to the tip, swirling it around the head. "Up and down. Everywhere."

"Fuck, yes," Nick growled.

"Filthy man with a filthy mouth. Clearly I need to scrub harder."

He reached a hand between her legs, parting and stroking her. Ida squirmed against his fingers, sighing in delight as she continued to pleasure him. Her hands worked him harder and faster, until an incoherent sound broke from his throat.

"Ida, please," he begged. "I need you."

She abandoned the soap and shifted to take him inside of her, riding his thrusts, controlling the speed and the angle. Water sloshed from the tub.

"Installing. One of. These," Nick choked out. "Today."

"Yes," Ida gasped, rocking faster, feeling the tension nearing its apex.

Nick clutched her, matching every motion, moving as if he were a part of her, as if they had been made to be one.

"Love you. So much."

Ida threw her head back and let the orgasm take her, floating on the bliss, feeling and hearing Nick's satisfaction around her and inside her. When the climax had spent itself, she sank into the water, sagging against his chest, weary and content.

"I love you, too."

He stroked her hair. "Bedroom, bathroom, dressing chamber. What other rooms will I have to redesign to account for our amorous exploits, do you think?"

"All of them. Except my workshop. Though I suppose you must design that regardless."

He laughed and kissed her cheek. This was perfect, here in his arms, her body warmed by the water and her heart ablaze with love. They snuggled together in silence, sharing soft kisses and gentle smiles.

The rattle of the door jarred her from her reverie. Before she could even move, her father stormed into the room, shouting something about debauchery and honor.

"For goodness' sake," she shouted back, "why must you all insist upon intruding on my privacy? All I wanted was time alone for a bath."

"You are clearly *not* alone."

The look on her father's face was positively murderous. Her mother, however, was beaming.

"You had damn well better marry her, Sharpe," Sir Mortimer snarled, "or I'll have your head, earl or no."

"There is no need to fuss, Papa," Ida said. "We have been engaged for a month and will soon be married."

"Can't be soon enough."

Beneath the water, she laced her fingers through Nick's. "Well, then, how does tomorrow work for you?"

XXVII

To Have and to Hold

The next day

GOOD GOD, HIS FAMILY WAS ENORMOUS. Nick didn't even recognize some of the faces in the crowd, let alone know their names. He may have been able to hazard a guess as to whether the strangers came from the prolific Masterson side or his mother's still more fecund relations, but then only because of who they were sitting with. Most amazingly, they were all here, filling the church, on such short notice. Maybe he *was* related to half of London.

If anyone was missing, he couldn't tell, except for the one face that meant the most to him. He scanned the congregation again. His mother smiled at him from the front of the pack. Nick fidgeted with his cufflinks.

"Wedding day jitters, Sharpe?"

Nick turned to face Ayleston. "No." The energy humming in his veins stemmed more from impatience than anything else. He longed for Ida to be his, not only by their mutual agreement, but in the eyes of God and man. "I'm eager to see my bride."

"Ah. Of course. I know you sent it weeks ago, but I haven't

186

yet had the chance to thank you for your report. Most of your troublemakers have been rounded up and locked away in prison or asylums. That man you called Thin-Face? Ex-military, once an intelligence agent in India. Later worked for the Imperial Potions Company. They fired him several months ago. It is believed he recruited the rogue soldiers working with him. Lady Holbeck, I'm afraid, has vanished without a trace. Gone into seclusion, people say, as a result of her husband's violent death."

"Violent death at her own hands," Nick scoffed.

"We will keep an eye out for her. As for the potions crisis, we have taken your recommendation and now have professionals looking into the matter."

Nick's gaze drifted to the candle-lit sconces around the church. A part of him would be happy to see potions vanish entirely. He was counting his temperance in weeks now and hoped to soon make it months. He knew, though, that the loss of potions would devastate the economy. He had already seen signs of lost jobs and closing businesses. He couldn't wish for the world to suffer merely to spare himself. He couldn't wish for Ida's brilliant business to die just as it was beginning.

"Send as many spies as you like," he said, "so long as you don't send me. I'm finished with investigations and danger."

"You made that quite clear, my boy. Your financial contribution to the cause was most generous. Combined with my resources and the funds authorized by Parliament, we could afford to send our best man."

"A loyal man, I hope. Someone of good character."

"Precisely why I did the choosing." Ayleston clapped Nick on the shoulder. "Congratulations, Nicholas. I will miss having your assistance, but I wish you all happiness."

Ayleston nodded goodbye and strode off to take the seat beside Nick's mother. The two clasped hands, chatted, and laughed, as loving siblings ought. Nick looked away, fighting envy. He'd known Anna was unlikely to be here, but her absence still left a gnawing emptiness in his gut.

Or perhaps that was the result of breaking his fast with nothing but coffee. Damn. He should have eaten something. Ida would have made him eat something. He looked out over the heads of the assembled crowd, toward the door where she would be entering at any moment.

Something solid rammed into him from behind and he staggered to keep his balance. A pair of slender arms wrapped around his waist, short gloves only half-concealing the familiar crescent-shaped birthmark on the left wrist.

"Anna." He spun around and crushed her to his chest. "You made it."

She hugged him for a long moment before stepping back and swatting at him playfully. Amber eyes that matched his own smiled up at him from her pretty, oval-shaped face. She wore her dark hair in its usual simple knot, but stray tendrils had come loose during her travels. Or had been knocked loose due to amorous exploits with her beloved husband. If it was the latter, Nick didn't want to know.

"Did you really think I would miss your wedding?" Anna asked. "We drove all night. We have exhausted all the fuel and the prices have become ridiculous, so I don't know how we will drive back. Perhaps we'll spend some time in London."

"Please do. I would like you to get to know Ida. I think you two will get along famously."

"Well, I'm certainly not leaving until I've spoken with her at least a few times. I'm dying of curiosity, Nick. She must be something to have gotten you all turned upside-down in so short a time."

He grinned. "She may well be a force of nature. She swept into my life without warning and I was powerless to resist her."

Her eyes twinkled. "Oh, you're in a bad way, brother. I can't wait to see you two together. And once the guests have gone, you are going to sit down and tell me everything. Between your telegrams that were barely a sentence and mother's Dickensian prose, it has proven impossible to piece together the truth of your real-life melodrama. Either a scandalous woman was ruining you, or you were ruining her. Then someone was in danger, but I never did ascertain which of you it was."

"Both of us. I used the rabbit."

Anna jumped in surprise. "No."

"I swear it. The weapon saved my life. I have no plans to restuff him with anything other than what ought to go inside a toy. I'm done with potions of all sorts."

She nodded thoughtfully. "I can respect that. But if you do ever again find yourself in danger, brother, you let me know at once. Nick the girl bear is still armed, and I'll happily sacrifice her to save my family."

Nick hugged his sister once again. "I love you, Anna. Thank you for rushing to be here for me. It means the world. And I promise to tell you the whole story, from beginning to end." His mouth twitched up into yet another broad smile. "Or, rather, Ida will tell you the whole story. She is a far better talker than I. She will give you details that I won't even remember I had forgotten."

Anna slipped from his grasp. "And she'll probably know the names of the people you encountered."

Nick shuddered. "Oh, God, the name problem. You are going to have great fun at my expense, I'm afraid."

"Excellent! I can hardly wait. Now I must go find a seat, because your bride has just appeared."

Anna darted off, but Nick couldn't have said what direction she went. His eyes were riveted on Ida. She dazzled in her blue and pink dress, a picture of elegance and happiness. White flowers decorated her hair, a matching bouquet clutched in her hands. The Sharpe diamonds glittered at her throat. Her cheeks glowed and her smile shone bright as a thousand candles.

The congregation rose and music swelled as Ida began her slow march to the altar. The breath whooshed from his lungs.

Wetness pricked at the corners of his eyes. This was really happening. He was marrying the woman he loved more than life itself. Their eyes met, linking them one to the other across the length of the church. A single tear overflowed, leaving a trail of moisture down Nick's cheek. He made no move to wipe it away or hide it. He would have no shame in his joy.

At long last, she stood before him, her own eyes bright and misty, sparking a second upwelling of emotion.

"Ida mine," he murmured. "I am yours. Forever."

"Dearly beloved," the priest began.

The words faded to a rhythmic backdrop to the paradise that was Ida's adoring smile. Before he knew it, Nick was pledging to love, comfort, honor, and keep her.

The priest turned to Ida. "Wilt thou have this man to be thy wedded husband, to live together after God's ordinance in the holy estate of Matrimony? Wilt thou obey him, and serve him, love, honor, and keep him, in sickness and in health; and, forsaking all others, keep thee only unto him, so long as ye both shall live?"

"I will," she declared. Then, "Except for the obeying bit."

All color drained from the minister's face.

"Keep going," Nick hissed. He would allow nothing and no one to stop this marriage.

"Er, y-yes. Um… Who, uh, who giveth this woman to be married to this man?"

Ida's father presented her, giving Nick a stony look. With any luck, his temper would cool once the ceremony had ended. Though after being caught naked in a tub with the man's daughter, Nick supposed he was fortunate not to have a gun pointed at his back.

He took Ida's right hand in his own and made his vows to her, his voice thick with emotion.

Ida's fingers squeezed his. Blinking back tears, she said, in a voice clear and firm, "I, Ida, take thee, Nicholas, to be my wedded husband, to have and to hold from this day forward, for better for worse, for richer for poorer, in sickness and in health, to love, cherish, and to *protect*, till death us do part, according to God's holy ordinance; and thereto I give thee my troth."

Nick had at least two cousins with connections to the newspaper industry. He and Ida would be all over the gossip rags tomorrow: the radical Earl of Sharpe and his scandalous, disobedient, feminist wife. No doubt his mother would clip all the articles and carefully preserve them for future generations to snicker at. Which suited Nick just fine. He slipped the pink heart ring onto the fourth finger of Ida's left hand.

He spoke again, his words an ardent growl. "With this ring I thee wed, with my body I thee worship."

The service continued on, but the only remaining portion that Nick heeded was, "man and wife." Their fingers would not untwine. He couldn't tear his eyes from her face. How had he gotten so damn lucky? He could stand there and bask in her perfection for all time.

"Nick."

He blinked at her.

"Kiss me, silly."

He bent down and pressed a chaste kiss to her lips, that brief touch sparking a rush of hot desire for what was yet to come.

"I love you."

"I love you, too, *husband*."

The smile she bestowed upon him nearly made him haul her against him and give her a kiss that would cause more than one of his delicately-inclined aunts to swoon. Ida stepped back just in time to prevent such a disaster and took hold of his arm with a possessive grip.

"Are all these people coming to your house for the wedding breakfast? Er, *our* house, I mean?" she asked as they made their way out to his waiting carriage.

"I assume so. Most will simply stop in, grab a bite of cake, and leave. I ordered cake from three different bakers because of the short notice. I hope it will be enough."

"I hope we have a chance to eat some. I understand we have to spend most of our time greeting people and accepting congratulations."

"They had better save us some cake. I'm famished."

"Didn't you eat anything before coming to church?"

"Only coffee."

Ida rolled her eyes. "How did you ever manage without me?"

"Badly."

He handed her up into the coach and climbed in behind her. "Shall I request the driver take a leisurely route back to my house? I entirely understand if you need time to prepare yourself before confronting my untold numbers of cousins. I don't even know all of their names."

Ida laughed. "Seeing as how you didn't know *my* name until you were practically in my bed this is not surprising in the least."

Nick moved to sit beside her, draping an arm around her shoulders. "Ah, but I know your name now, Ida, Lady Sharpe."

Her lips grazed his cheek. "A leisurely ride does sound nice. Though we can't ignore your stomach. How hungry are you?"

He caught her chin in his hand, tilting her head to gaze deeply into her eyes. "Ravenous."

One hour later, the happy but disheveled couple alighted from the vehicle and ascended the steps of the home that was now theirs. Nick held his wife close, breathing in the strawberry perfume that she had selected especially for him.

"I find I no longer care whether they've saved us any cake," he said.

His stomach grumbled and she raised a skeptical brow. "Really?"

"Absolutely. I'd rather have Berries any day." He scooped her up off her feet and carried her across the threshold. Home at last.

Epilogue

London
November, 1882

"LADY SHARPE!"

Ida sighed and set down her book. A woman swamped in layers of red plaid barged into the drawing room, her bustle wobbling as she attempted to run in her tight, heavy garments. Nick's portly butler trailed after her, red-faced and out of breath.

"Lady Whitmore to see you, my lady," he wheezed.

Ida thanked him with a forced smile. She ought to have told the staff that she wasn't at home to callers. These early months were a critical time for her burgeoning business, and the combination of her workload and her impending motherhood left her waging a constant war with fatigue. She valued these restful moments and disliked any interruption that wasn't her husband.

Lady Whitmore plonked down onto a chair opposite the couch where Ida sat. "Oh, Lady Sharpe, thank goodness you are available today. I'm desperate. Absolutely desperate!"

Ida studied her visitor, trying to recall when they had been introduced. It must have been at a party, because she certainly had never called here before. Unless she was one of Nick's cousins. Ida didn't know half of them yet, though she was relatively certain she now knew more of their names than he did.

"You are *the* Ida, are you not?" Lady Whitmore asked. "Of Perfumes by Ida? I sent one of my women to purchase two of your scented handkerchiefs some weeks ago, and now I simply cannot do without. Six washings they've gone through. Six! And the scent is as fresh and perfect as the day they were purchased. I must have a dozen more in every color, in scents of rose, lavender, and violet, and I need them in time for Christmas. You see, I had planned to distribute bottles of Mr. Quimby's new Fantastical Flavorant, which he said would turn ordinary water into 'exotic elixirs of fruity delight,' but in truth the water simply tastes as if someone may once have waved a piece of fruit in its general direction."

Ida swallowed back a laugh. Alfred's newest get-rich-quick scheme was as hopeless as the last, but at least this one was funny.

"You must help me, Lady Sharpe. My Christmas ball will be absolutely ruined without memorable favors for all the ladies. Your perma-fume handkerchiefs are my only hope. I also must have an additional set made for myself based on my own personal scent. Please tell me it is not hopeless."

"A rush job of that size is possible, though it would incur an additional charge," Ida replied. "As would a custom scent."

"Of course, of course. Price is no obstacle. I must have those handkerchiefs."

"And you will have them. Let me fetch my notebook and we can chat over tea."

Lady Whitmore seized Ida's hand and squeezed it. "Thank you, Lady Sharpe. You are such a dear!"

Two pots of tea and half-a-dozen chocolate biscuits later, Ida grinned down at her neat list of details and pricing for the largest order she had ever taken on. It would mean putting off her next experiment until after the new year, but she would absolutely trade that for the boost this would give her reputation.

"This has been so wonderful, Lady Sharpe," her new friend gushed. "I was rather shocked by the whole notion of a lady doing business, you know, but now that we have talked it really does make great sense. Why, I would much prefer if all such dealings involved tea and genteel women! And you are just the unique sort of person to set the trend, what with your short hair and your peculiar husband. Did he truly decorate this entire house himself? I heard that Lord Lakewood has hired him to redesign every room in his new townhouse. Hired him! For pay!"

"All true. Lord Sharpe has very modern ideas about business and gentlemanly professions."

"Well, I'm not certain what to think of it all, but this room is charming. The furniture seems rather large and masculine for a drawing room, but the pink color softens everything."

"Thank you. I'm very fond of it. I much prefer the heavier furniture, because I want both ladies and gentlemen to feel welcomed here. If I had dainty little pieces, my husband might never sit down for fear of breaking them."

"So good of you to think of me, darling."

Ida's head swiveled in the direction of that lovely, deep voice and she sprang from her seat. "Nick, you are home! I thought Lakewood might keep you forever."

He crossed the room and kissed her cheek. "I had to talk him out of purchasing the most unsightly chandelier. It looked like something out of a Parisian brothel." His eyes darted to their guest. "Er, not that I have ever visited such a place."

"Nick, you know Lady Whitmore, don't you? She has placed a large order for my perma-fume handkerchiefs."

Lady Whitmore allowed Nick to bow over her hand, then she turned and caught Ida up in a sudden embrace, kissing the air to either side of her cheek in Continental fashion.

"Thank you, my dear. I'm so pleased I could do business with you. And I may be in touch with you, Lord Sharpe, about my own drawing room."

"I would be happy to discuss it, Lady—"

"Whitmore," Ida whispered.

"Whitmore."

"Excellent. Good day to you both."

The moment Lady Whitmore was out the door, Nick closed it behind her and turned the key.

"So. A large order?"

"The largest." Ida couldn't help bouncing. "I'm so excited! Nervous, but excited."

Nick pulled her into his arms. "Congratulations, love. You deserve success after all your hard work." He kissed her neck, unfastening the buttons at the back of her dress to tug the collar lower. "I was dismayed, however, to discover that my lovely wife is a liar."

"Am I? What did I say?"

Nick backed her up against the fainting couch. Ida sank onto the cushions and he lowered himself over her, his eager hands dragging her neckline down and her skirts up.

"You didn't tell her the real reason we purchased such sturdy furniture."

Ida wound her arms around his neck and pressed her mouth to his in a long, luxurious kiss.

"I can't tell her that," she said, when they at last came up for air. "The only thing more scandalous than a lord and lady engaging in trade is a lord and lady passionately in love with one another."

"Well, then, my scandalous lady, please allow your scandalous lord to demonstrate the depths of his passionate love."

Ida pulled him close, savoring his heat, his scent, and the weight of his hard body against her own. Wanting him. Loving him.

"It would be my pleasure."

The End

Historical Note

THE VICTORIAN ERA saw huge advancements in travel, with the rise of railroads, steamships, and even the beginning of the automobile. Long-distance travel became less dangerous, faster, and affordable to a much wider number of people. In 1873, Jules Verne published *Around the World in Eighty Days*, a travel adventure very much based on the available methods of transportation at the time. In fact, by 1889, when Nellie Bly replicated an around-the-world trip, she managed it in only seventy-two days.

Around the World in Eighty Days was also first published in English in 1873, and was popular enough that Nick and Ida would likely know of it and possibly have read it. Ida's original route to India follows a very similar path to the one in the book, along the major railway lines of the time.

All of Ida's guidebooks are real. The *Baedeker's Guides* were the first popular travel guides, giving travelers a wealth of information about cities, sights, places to stay, and methods of transportation. The 1881 *Paris and Environs* provided me with such details as the price and type of wine that Nick and Ida drink and the number of theaters in Paris.

Ida's other primary guidebook is *Bradshaw's Through Route Overland Guide to India*. I used the 1884 edition of this guide to get period-accurate train and steamship timetables and routes from London all the way to Bombay (now properly known as Mumbai). This guide includes real advertisements for the supposed cure-all Chlorodyne (a mixture which included laudanum, cannabis, and chloroform) and the invalid chairs Ida teases Nick about. The seasickness cures Ida offers, such as creosote, come directly from this guide, as does her suggestion of pale ale and oranges as safe foods in Alexandria.

Finally, the brief glimpses of monkeys in India come from my own wonderful visit to that country in June of 2018 and the "two very sacred but apparently very mischievous monkeys" noted by the Prince of Wales in his account of his visit to India: *From Pall Mall to the Punjab*—another book Ida is likely to have known of.

Digitized copies of these resources can be found at the following sites:

Baedeker's Guides:
https://archive.org/details/baedeckers

Bradshaw's Guide:
https://books.google.com/books?id=mUNFAQAAMAAJ

From Pall Mall to the Punjab:
https://archive.org/details/frompallmalltop01gaygoog

About the Author

CATHERINE STEIN started reading at age two, when her mother noticed that she could tell the difference between words that started with the same letter. Ever since, she has wandered around with a book in her hand, her backpack, her purse, or even tucked down the back of her pants. A few years after she began to read, she also began to write, spending the majority of her school career writing non-school-related stories in her notebooks. Now she writes sassy, sexy stories set during the Victorian and Edwardian eras and full of action, adventure, magic, and fantastic technologies.

Catherine lives in Michigan with her husband and three rambunctious girls. She can often be found dressed in clothing that was purchased at a Renaissance Festival, drinking copious amounts of tea.

Visit Catherine online at
www.catsteinbooks.com
and join her VIP mailing list.

Follow her on Twitter @catsteinbooks,
or like her page on Facebook @catsteinbooks.

Also by Catherine Stein

How to Seduce a Spy

A barmaid with a rare talent.
A spy on a mission.
A love neither can resist.

Available at your favorite online retailer.

www.catsteinbooks.com

· · · ⛱ · · ·

Thank you so much for reading.
If you enjoyed the book and are so inclined, I would love for
you to leave a review. Happy readers make an author's day!

I love hearing from readers,
so feel free to contact me on social media, or email:

catherine@catsteinbooks.com